CW00867721

A Reckoning

A Reckoning

Unflinching Book IV

Stuart G. Yates

Also by Stuart G. Yates

- Unflinching

- In The Blood

- To Die In Glory

- Varangian

- Varangian 2 (King of the Norse)

- Burnt Offerings

- Whipped Up

- Splintered Ice

- The Sandman Cometh

- Roadkill

- Tears in the Fabric of Time

- Lament for Darley Dene

Acknowledgments

A big thank you once gain to Alex of BOO BOOKS, whose great professionalism and attention to detail always leaves me breathless

This one is for Honey, with thanks, for the happiness shared

Chapter One

The moment Dan Stoakes discovered the vein of silver in the bank of a tributary of the South Platte River, he fell down in the dirt of the muddy bank and cried with joy. Careless of the water lapping over his cord pants, when he clambered to his feet, deliriously happy, he slipped and fell head first to the ground. He rolled over and peered towards the sky. "I've died and gone to heaven," he said aloud, bursting into more tears. For five long years he had toiled in this little known part of the river system, wary of Indians and strangers but never encountering either. He rarely ventured into the nearby town of Twin Buttes, and then only to get supplies. He kept himself to himself and did his best not to make eye contact with anyone. An almost unhealthy belief in what lay beside the river pushed him towards ever greater efforts.

Up until now, his precautions seemed to have worked. Nobody knew of his progress. And now, of course, success.

Alone in his little camp, made from nothing more than an old piece of tarpaulin, he laboured at the riverbanks, following his instinct and knowledge of rock formations. This one particular cold morning, when his handpick prized away a heavy clump of mud and shale, he paused in disbelief at the silver trail threading its way through the exposed bedrock, and for a moment believed he had slipped into a dream world. To verify the truth of his efforts, he continued chipping away to discover more of the vein. There was no doubting his eyes or any other sense – he had struck silver.

For the remainder of the morning, he staked out his claim. The stakes, prepared more than four years before, he fetched from where he'd stacked them in the far corner of his camp, waiting for the day. Well, the day was here and he worked feverishly to finish pounding them into the hard-packed soil. Satisfied, he set to making a monument out of a collection of stones and boulders to identify the location. Finally, he gathered some samples into a leather pouch to take down into the town assay office. He paused, eyeing his work with grim satisfaction, took a long drink from his canteen and packed up his mule ready for the journey.

He sang as he rode, a tuneless rendition of something his mother used to hum when he was just a toddler. It helped ease the tedium of the trek down to Twin Buttes.

Cutting across a ford in the river, he meandered along the valley, skirting woodland and rocky high ground until he reached the ancient trail which marked the way to town. He did all he could to keep his mind from his discovery, but every now and then the enormity of what had happened hit him and he would emit a high-pitched cackle, giving himself over to uncontained joy at what it might mean for himself and his family. A single daughter, from a marriage long since annulled, lived a quiet life in Kansas City, bringing up her young son alone. A miscreant husband, having realised life with Melody was not one he wished to continue, especially after the boy was born, left her to find his fortune in New York. That was some four years previously, and Bradford Milligan had not been heard of since. Dan felt elation when the news reached him and, with the promises of riches so close, the future seemed bright – for his daughter, grandson and himself.

Now, rolling into town, Dan steered his mount towards the lone saloon Twin Buttes possessed and eased his weary body from the saddle. He stretched his back before stepping inside, licking his lips with anticipation, and crossed to the bar.

The room was small, cramped, the floor covered with sawdust and a scattering of rushes. The interior decorations, uniformly grey in colour, appeared tired and in need of refurbishment. Cleaning might help, for the place smelled of musty clothes too long in the cupboard edged with traces of urine, human or otherwise. Either way, the aroma stuck in the back of Dan's throat, urging him to want to down the whisky he ordered from the diminutive barman in one. "Don't often see you in here," the barman said, putting another shot of whisky in front of Dan.

Dan gazed at the amber liquid, imagining its taste trickling down into his stomach. "Don't often come in here, that's why." He lifted the drink, inspecting it closely, savouring the moment. Then, in a sudden movement of his arm, he threw the entire glassful down his throat. Gasping, he bent forward, holding onto the counter edge with his free hand and shaking his head. "Hot dang, that's good."

"Is it your birthday?"

Shaking his head again, Dan grinned. "No, a celebration of an altogether different kind." He patted his shoulder bag containing the silver sample. "Life changing." He gestured with the glass for a refill, which this time went down with a good deal more care. Snapping a dollar on the counter, when he finished his drink he turned on his heels and went outside.

His next stop was at the newly opened telegraph office. He scrawled out a few lines and slid the paper across to the operator, who twisted his mouth, sighed and tapped out the message. Dan leaned on the counter, head filled with something thick and heavy, and thought he was going to be sick. Not waiting for confirmation, he paid his due and quickly went outside.

Swaying, he waited until the cold air cleared his head before tramping across to the assayer's office. "Damned whisky," he muttered to himself and stepped up to the office door. Finding it locked, he craned his neck to survey the building, hoping to find some clue as to when it might open again, but the wooden walls and blacked-out windows gazed back at him in silence. Disappointed, he decided to try the bank in hope of finding some information.

Inside the small, cramped confines of the bank, a teller, bent over a large ledger, peered at Ben over the top of his glasses. "I know you."

"You should, I've lived around these parts for more than two years."

"Well, that might be it, but from the look of you and," he sniffed, "the *smell*, I think I'd know if you were a regular customer. You ain't."

"I was hoping to find the assay office open."

"Assay office? Don't believe that has been open for quite a while. Years maybe. You have some items to assess?"

"You might say that. Where would I find the assay officer?"

The teller blew out his cheeks and sat back, contemplating Dan for a moment. "That would be Arnold Schiller, I reckon. Half Moon Street, above the haberdashers there, which his brother and wife own. That would be your best bet. He is retired now, I do believe. Why are you so keen to find him?"

"I'm wondering – if I *don't* find him, or if something else has happened, might I deposit my bag here in the bank?" He brought up the said bag and placed it on the desk front.

The teller leaned forward, pressing his lips together. "Well, there's a possibility, I suppose. What's in it?"

Dan chuckled and picked up his bag again. "I'll let you know – if Mr Schiller ain't at home."

A hard look, followed by a snappy "I see," and the teller returned to his ledger, leaving Dan to wander outside and make his way down to Half Moon Street.

As things turned out, Dan did find Schiller at home and, after recounting his tale, persuaded the assay officer to cross over to his office and open it up. Dan stood in the dull half-light whilst Schiller strained to open first one, then the other pair of shutters. The light streamed in, revealing a dust-encrusted interior, everything grey, forlorn. Schiller took his time, assembling a set of scales, arranging the collection of weights and then examined the contents of Dan's bag. After much grunting and chewing of his lip, he finally sat back and declared the metal genuine. "You have struck silver, sir," and presented Dan with the appropriate papers to complete.

Emerging from the office some two hours later, Dan did not notice the two men loitering across the road. Nor was he aware of them leading their horses out into Mainstreet to follow him out of town and back to his encampment.

If he had noticed them, Dan may have lived.

Chapter Two

Simms spent his morning sweeping out the sheriff's office at Glory. Stepping inside, he read again, for the umpteenth time, the telegram the Pinkerton office in Chicago had sent him the previous day. They wanted him to report to headquarters, to discuss suggestions put forward by the new mayor of Glory, Doctor Grove. They also wanted him to bring in the money, something Simms had put off for long enough. The original idea was to secure it at Fort Bridger, under the watchful eye of Colonel Johnstone, but trouble was again brewing in the north of the Territory. With a Mormon splinter group growing more belligerent with every passing day, the army's orders were clear – suppress any hint of trouble which may impair the negotiated settlement made between Brigham Young, the Mormon leader, and the President.

"I brought you some corn bread."

Simms looked up to see Mrs. Miller standing before him, well-kitted out in powder blue dress and matching bonnet. She held a tray, covered by a white, embroidered cloth. She smiled and lifted the cover to reveal half a dozen pieces of soft, moist bread. Simms leaned forward, eyes closed, and breathed in the aroma.

"My, they smell good, Mrs. Miller."

"Call me Laura," she said, stepping up onto the boardwalk. She studied the broom in the detective's hands. "You should get someone else to do that."

He blanched a little, looking away, awkward, "There is no one else … Laura. Thank you for the bread." He propped the broom against the wall and took the tray from her.

"You should have someone, Sheriff. A man like you, so busy and all, you need someone to share the load."

He opened his mouth to speak, but couldn't find any words, so he simply gave a small laugh.

"I could make you some coffee. Coffee and corn bread is a wonderful combination."

"Mrs Miller, I—"

"*Laura.*"

"Yes, Laura. I, er, I have quite a lot to do this morning. I need to tidy this place up before I leave."

"You're leaving?"

He caught something in her voice, a shred of alarm perhaps, and he quickly continued, "Only temporary, you understand. I'll be back in a week, perhaps less."

"Well, even more reason for me to make that coffee."

She set about brewing the coffee whilst Simms did his best to keep his mind on sweeping the floor, but his eyes constantly drifted towards her slim waist, those tumbling curls, the random sprinkling of freckles across her cheeks and nose.

They sat down, Simms behind his desk, Laura Miller beside the wood burner, sipping hot coffee. The lawman munched on a piece of bread, grateful for having something to do whilst her eyes burned into him.

"It must be hard for you," she said at last, her voice sounding overly loud in the confines of the small office.

He arched a single eyebrow. "Hard? No, no, once I get back from Bridger I shall swear in a deputy or two before beginning to look through what needs to be done."

"I didn't mean your work, Mr Simms. I meant your life. Moving backwards and forwards from here to Bovey, holding down your shared responsibilities, living out in your ranch house, all alone. I know what it is like to be alone, Mr Simms. My husband was taken two years ago this spring. I understand your wife, too, was taken by the fever?"

Pausing with a piece of bread hovering close to his mouth, Simms forced down a swallow and, no longer hungry, returned the slice to the tray, sat and stared. "It was the birth that killed her, Mrs. Miller. No doubt she was weakened by the fever before she went into labour, but ..." His voice trailed away and an awkward silence followed, during which neither looked at each other, Simms preferring to focus his attention on the crumbs sprinkled across his desk.

"Listen," she said suddenly, slapping her knees and standing up, "why don't you come to dinner? My cooking is renowned throughout the entire town, Mr Simms, and you won't find a better—"

"That's kind of you, it surely is, but like I told you – I have to leave for Bridger."

"When you get back, I mean. The first Sunday of your return, what do you say?"

"Well, I ..." He looked up into her eyes. Green eyes, flecked with hints of gold. Heat rose to his jawline and he squirmed in his chair, staring into his empty coffee cup for something to do. "That's very kind of you."

"We shouldn't dwell on the past, Mr Simms. We should do all we can to move forward."

"Should we?"

"I believe so. If we don't, we become immersed in grief, regret, thoughts of what might have been." She stood and moved to the desk. "I'm not saying forget, Mr Simms, but we should try and—"

"Live with it?"

Laura Miller averted her eyes, twiddling her thumbs. "Time. Time eases the pain, but the memories remain. The *good* memories. My Tom was a kind, loving man. We married back in Fifty-One. Five years we were together. I often wonder where those five years went, and I struggle sometimes to recall what we did, where we went, most of it being little more than a blur. But he is still here," she put her fist against her breast, "and he always will be. Such thoughts won't bring him back, of course. Nothing will, but I believe it is important, for my own wellbeing, to move on." Smiling, she gathered up her purse and put out her hand. "The first Sunday then?"

Simms half-rose, taking her slim, soft hand, not knowing whether to shake it or kiss it, social etiquette not being a strong point of his. She saved him by giving his fingers a squeeze, then turned and left.

Slumping back into his chair, Simms blew out a long sigh. The last woman he'd allowed into his heart almost got him killed. Although he did not believe Mrs. Milligan harboured such dark desires, nevertheless Simms had promised himself not to succumb to the charms of a pretty woman again. And Mrs. Miller was pretty, no doubts about that. But then, so was Tabatha, and Tabatha wanted him dead.

Chapter Three

Returning to his camp, Dan tied up his old mule and sat down amongst the rocks and scree. He didn't care about the discomfort. Years of living outdoors, in all sorts of weathers whilst he scrabbled around searching for precious metals, meant his body had grown well-conditioned to anything nature threw at him. He stretched out his legs and pulled out the papers he'd signed back at the assay office and grinned like a little boy. All the years of struggle, all the disappointments, the constant setbacks, all of it worth it, for now he was on the brink of something big. Once Melody came out, they could discuss in which direction their lives might lead. She was a good girl, but with her husband gone, she struggled, as most did, to make ends meet. Now, none of that mattered. Only good times waited for them all to enjoy.

Rousing himself, he set to making a fire. He put an old iron pot, filled with water, onions and sweet potatoes, on the flames and lay back as the stew gently bubbled. He peered up to a sky of uniform blue, not a cloud to break up the view. In a few months, the heat would rise, as it always did, and life would change. Winter proved hard, as always, but summer too held its own particular dangers. But for now, out here with no worries, he allowed himself to relax and, before long, with his eyelids growing heavy, he snuggled into his coat and dozed.

The sizzling of the pot, accompanied by an acrid smell, brought him back to full consciousness and he sat up. Stretching out his arms, he went over to the fire and stared into what was left of his stew. "Ah, damn it," he spat. The water had all boiled away, leaving the vegetables a congealed, dark brown mass on the bottom of the pan. He doubted he could save two spoonfuls but made a brave try of it nevertheless. Scooping up the burnt remnants, he found a couple of pieces of potato and, keeping his mouth half open to allow the cool air to circulate inside, he tenderly munched them down.

It was then he heard the footfall.

He did his best not to react; instead he fanned his mouth in an exaggerated way, giving himself time to check how far away his shotgun was. Perhaps six paces it stood propped against a tree, alongside the bivouac. He might make it. Then again, he might not. So he stopped, put the pan down on the ground, and turned.

Two men stood before him, heavy set, dressed in long over-coats, black hats, faces ruddy with the cold air. Neither spoke, their dark eyes never blinking. The world waited.

Dan sucked in a breath. "Howdy," he said and nodded to the remains of the burnt stew. "I'd offer you some, but it's … Well, let's just say it ain't all that palatable."

A sudden gust of wind rampaged through the tiny camp, sending up a swirl of dead, fallen leaves and particles of dust. It ended almost as soon as it began, but something about it brought a stab of fear to Dan's insides and he quailed, taking a quick glance towards his shotgun. "Fellas," he managed, voice quivering, "I'm not sure what it is you're wanting, but whatever it is, I ain't got it."

"The deeds."

The two words crackled, filled with threat. Of what, Dan could not say, but he could guess. He watched the way their arms hung loose at their sides, so close to the revolvers holstered there. A loud swallow before he threw out his arms, "Fellas, I ain't sure what you mean by *deeds*."

"This place," said the spokesman, casting a glance around the camp, ticking off the hammered-in stakes with a single nod of his head, "this claim. How much is it worth, do you figure?"

"Worth? Hell, I doubt if it is anything more than a couple of hundred." Dan licked his lips, trying to buy some time. He climbed to his feet and took a small, sideways step. "Fellas, I'm not sure where you've got your information, but I swear to you, there ain't much of anything left around these parts. You must know that. What there is couldn't feed a family for a year. I promise."

"Show us."

Frowning, Dan chanced another glance towards his shotgun. In that single look, he knew he would never make it. His shoulders sagged. "How did you know where to find me?"

"We saw you in town. Followed you. Now, show us."

"It ain't worth it, fellas. If I had found anything of value, I'd have—"

The single, metallic clunk of a gun hammer being cocked caused Dan to turn his gaze to the spokesman, and the gun filling his hand. The man snarled, "Now."

Defeated, Dan sank within himself. Shaking his head, he led them along the stream, to the place where he'd dug through the surface rock. The little mound of stones stood where he'd built it, a monument to his hopes and dreams, all of them now dashed. He stifled a cry of anguish and pointed with a trembling hand towards where he'd mined. "There. It runs through the side of the hill, but I don't know how deep."

The second man grunted and went over to investigate. He scrabbled around in the earth for a few moments before turning again to grin at his companion. "Silver."

The other returned the grin, bobbing his head with triumph. He looked across at Dan. "You did well, old-timer. How can we ever thank you?" Then he fired the gun, the bullet taking Dan in the side of the neck, blowing him backwards into the stream, where he writhed and gargled, blood welling from the wound to mingle with the gently rolling water. Within a few seconds, he grew still, his body rolling over, taken down stream by the current, soon to disappear.

Chapter Four

In the late afternoon, he set out across the plain towards Fort Bridger. Simms followed the ancient trail snaking through the land, a trail so old nobody knew of its origins. Some said it was an old Ute pathway. If it was, they no longer used it. Only pilgrims and homesteaders did so now. He passed a few, plodding along in slow, weary processions, sometimes a dozen or more wagons snaking by. Some acknowledged him, some grabbed for their rifles, most simply kept their eyes set firmly ahead. Simms wondered how many of them would make it.

On the second day, after a breakfast of salted biscuits and steaming coffee, he spotted a cluster of half-erected buildings and turned his horse towards them. Set in the shadow of a small mountain range, the jagged grey peaks soaring way above the tree line, the buildings were close to completion. Men laboured in the cold, their exertions rendering the need for coats unnecessary, their breath steaming in the sharp air. Approaching them at an easy gait, when he was within earshot, Simms pulled up his horse and leaned forward in his saddle, observing the workers hammering nails, fitting joists and securing wood panels for the walls. A broad, heavily built individual, sporting a black Derby hat, sauntered over. He smoked a cigar and regarded Simms with obvious wariness, eyes narrowed, coat pulled back to reveal a handgun holstered at his hip.

"Good day to you," he said, his accent strange, not unlike Martinson's, the Swedish merchant who continued to run a store and eating place just outside of Bovey, despite the mines having dried up years before.

Simms grunted, motioning towards the construction work. "Seems a mite strange to be building a home all the way out here."

The man tilted his head, cigar clamped between his teeth. "It's not a home, mister, it's a staging post. Now, if I could ask you what you—"

"A staging post? You mean, a stage will run through here?"

"A stagecoach, yes. What's your interest, mister?"

"I'm sheriff over in Glory," said Simms, emphasising the point by drawing back his coat to reveal the star pinned to his vest. He also made sure the man got a good glimpse of the Dragoon at his side.

The man munched on the cigar, punctuating his words with puffs of thick smoke. "I see. Well, my name is O'Shaughnessy, Liam O'Shaughnessy. You may have heard of me?"

Simms stared back, nothing stirring in his memory.

"Well," the man puffed up his chest, as well as his cigar. "Me and my colleagues have been hired by the stagecoach company as security for these here workers," he jerked a thumb behind him towards the men labouring away at the construction of the buildings, "so I'll be asking you to move on, if you don't mind." He grinned. "*Sheriff.*"

Another grunt, and Simms twisted around to survey the mountains, the various passes, outcrops and clumps of undergrowth which hyphenated the jagged rock face. "This is a dangerous area, Mr O'Shaughnessy. It would be my advice to post sentries, night and day. You have horses here, and Bannocks want horses."

"Bannocks? What in the hell are they?"

"Indians. There's a lot of Indians around here, and most of them are mean and desperate, so you'd best be prepared."

"Bah," O'Shaughnessy leaned to his right, pulling out the cigar, and spat into the dirt, "I ain't got no worries about Indians, Mister Sheriff. Only white folk looking for mischief." He fastened the cigar between his teeth again. "Of whatever kind."

Straightening himself in his saddle, Simms gave a final sweeping glance across the building site and sighed, "Well, all my best to you and I hope it all goes according to plan."

"Oh, it will. Don't you worry about that none."

"No, I won't." Simms doffed his hat and turned his horse away, a little riled at O'Shaughnessy's gruff manner, curious why he seemed so anxious for Simms to leave. He made a mental note to look through the records to see if there was anything pending on Mr Liam O'Shaughnessy and, if there was, he may well return for a second, more searching visit.

Chapter Five

There were enough of Dan's prospecting tools and equipment in the camp for both men to set about excavating the silver lode on the morning after they killed him. The killer sat on a boulder, reading through the papers, stumbling over some of the words, his mouth forming them silently. "Says nothing here about limitations of rights," he said at last, folding the papers and stuffing them inside his shirt.

"What in hell does that mean?" said the other, studying a gnarled and chipped spade.

"I'm guessing that means there is no legal impediment to our prospecting and developing the mine."

"Impediment? Jesus, Quincy, you sound like a damned lawyer."

Stretching out his legs, Quincy beamed, basking in the words of his friend, liking the idea of being thought of as a lawyer. "Hell, Charlie, I ain't even been to school, saving Miss Franklyn's Sunday School back in Oakley when I was nothing but a kid. All we learned there was how to tie our bootlaces and recite the Lord's Prayer."

"I ain't even been to no Sunday school," said Charlie, hefting the spade. "I reckon, if there is no *impediment*, we should set to it without delay. Other people might have the same idea as us."

"I doubt that. How could anyone else know?"

"The old-timer might have told people. We saw him at the bank. He may have been arranging a deposit for all we know. We need to be careful."

Grunting, Quincy stood up. "You might have something there, Charlie. We need to protect our investment. I know the folk who work at the bank. It might secure our position if we were to silence any tittle-tattles."

"And how do you plan on doing that?"

"I'll kill the bastards, that's what I'll do."

Quincy screwed up his mouth. "Seems a mite extreme, Quincy."

"Needs must. Let me ruminate on how best to do the deed. Hand me that pick, old friend, and I'll think it through whilst we're working."

They worked through the best part of the day, sweating despite the raw cold. Muscles burned and sinews strained as they hacked and dug, cutting through the rock, opening up the initial hole made by Dan until it was big enough to crawl through. They shored up the roof with timber cut from the surrounding trees, lit animal fat candles to enable them to continue in the gloom and prized out hunks of rock with lines of precious metal running through them.

By the early evening, both exhausted, they lay stretched out on the ground, quenching their thirst with water taken from the stream. They slept in the open, ignoring the cold, mindless of any dangers.

The following day they huddled around the meagre campfire Charlie managed to make, their bodies trembling with the cold, limbs aching with the previous day's exertions.

"We should take it slower," said Quincy. "If we continue at this rate, we'll end up killing ourselves."

"Every day we linger is another day someone else might come here. We can't delay, Quincy."

"Yeah, I know. And I've thought of something."

Charlie drew closer, intrigued.

"If I'm right, then the only people he would have told would be those in the bank. Now, tomorrow is Sunday, and everyone will be at church. So, we work through today and tomorrow, then on Monday we ride into town at daybreak, set ourselves to watch."

"Watch? Watch what?"

"The bank. When it opens, we stroll right on in and rob it."

Charlie's mouth fell open, perplexed. His eyes grew wide and then he cackled, dismissively. "Jeez, Quincy, we don't need no more money. With all this here silver we could buy the entire—"

"I don't mean we rob it for the money."

Charlie blinked a few times. "You're not making any sense at all, Quincy."

"I mean, we *pretend* we're robbing it, and as we do, I'll shoot them all dead."

"*What*? Are you out of your damned mind? We'll have an army of deputies tracking us down before the day is out!"

"We'll wear masks. No one'll know. We'll scoot back here and no one will ever think it's us, even if they do chase us, which I doubt."

Digging at the pathetic embers of the dying fire with his boot, Charlie shook his head. "I don't know, Quincy, it all sounds mighty hazardous. We don't even know if them tellers and such know anything about the silver."

"You said yourself we have to be careful."

"Yeah, I know, but – hot damn, Quincy, I never meant we should murder the whole goddamned lot of 'em."

"Well what else do you propose? We can't afford to take the risk."

"I got a better idea. One not so dangerous."

Now it was Quincy's turn to gape, bewildered. "*You* have a plan? Jesus, Charlie, I must be in a dream."

Charlie's face grew dark and serious. "Just 'cause I ain't ever been given the opportunity, don't mean I can't think things through, Quincy. My idea will work, and it'll mean no damned posse will come hunting for us."

Narrowing his eyes, features full of intrigue and pessimism, Quincy regarded his friend for a long time. "All right, Charlie. Tell me all about this fine plan of yours."

And Charlie did. By the time he was finished, Quincy, convinced, if not a little surprised, agreed to everything his friend said.

Chapter Six

The snow fell again, perhaps the final blast of the winter. Simms hoped so as he dismounted at the fort livery stable and led his horse to cover. The stable-boy did not speak, merely grunted when Simms pressed a coin in his hand. Swinging the saddle-bags over his shoulder, the detective tramped over to the line of wooden buildings set against the far wall of the fort. Soldiers milled around, many of them cleaning equipment and, in the square, a burly sergeant harangued a young, red-headed recruit. Simms paid them little heed and strode towards the officer's mess. A sentry on duty brought himself to attention, right arm barring Simms's path through the door.

"Sorry, sir, but you'll have to state your business."

"Name's Simms. I'm a Pinkerton Detective. Colonel Johnstone knows me well enough, if you'll announce me I'll—"

"Begging your pardon, but the Colonel is away from the fort at present, sir. Major Porter is in command until the Colonel's return."

"Very well, can you announce me to the Major, then?"

The sentry stiffened, growing nervous, uncertain. "He is presently engaged, sir."

Simms blew out a breath. "And how long will he be?"

"Difficult to say, sir."

Nodding, Simms turned and looked across the square. The fort, in a much better state of repair since the last time he visited, buzzed with not only soldiers but numerous workers, ranch hands, settlers and drifters. Most of those he saw were men, in varying modes of attire, but almost all were suffering from the severe cold. The new blizzard struck hard, taking everyone by surprise. It seemed most made their way to 'Clancy's Dining Room and Grill', which no doubt served as a welcome warming place for everyone.

"You have a safe around here, somewhere I can deposit valuables?"

"There's the paymaster's office." The soldier pointed across to the left. Simms eyed a worn-out looking building, built from brick. "Warrant officer Trent is the man to speak to."

"Obliged." Simms doffed his hat and turned to go. He paused, turning to regard the soldier, raising a single eyebrow. "You were ordered to stay out here?"

"Er, yes sir, I was. The Major … He likes his privacy."

"And how does his visitor leave his office? Through a back door?"

"Er, that would be the preferred exit, yes, sir."

Chuckling, Simms stepped down. "Best keep your mind off what's going on within, private. Such things can damage a young man's hearing."

Trent stood up after locking the safe and turned, smiling. "That's a lot of money, Detective. You planning on keeping it here for long?"

"Only until the Colonel returns, then he will take responsibility."

"Unfortunately, I have no way of telling how long he will be absent. Reports came in of some trouble close to the River. Seems a band of Utes attacked a Mormon settlement, carried off many of the women and children. Something has riled them and they are in a mean mood, so the Colonel has ridden off with two troops of men. We're all a tad nervous about it, as we have less than twenty armed men left to protect the fort."

"You think it might be attacked?"

"We can't tell. I hope to God not."

Simms grunted, rubbing his grizzled chin, deep in thought. "You had any news filtering through about the building of a stagecoach station, halfways between here and Bovey?"

Trent considered the question for a moment. "Nothing that I know of. I can check if you want me to? I know for certain Ben Holladay has been extending his mail routes through the Territory."

"I'd be obliged if you could confirm it for me, Officer."

"Can I ask why you're so interested?"

"Oh, just a feeling. I had some words with a none too considerate gentleman by the name of O'Shaughnessy. Wondered if there might be some papers on him."

"I'll check on that too."

Simms thanked the Warrant Officer and stepped back outside, buttoning his overcoat up to the chin in an attempt to keep out the cold. He failed and hurried across the square towards 'Clancy's'.

The heavy, smoke-filled air caused him to waver in the doorway. Already his eyes smarted and he squeezed them with the finger and thumb of his right hand.

"You'll get used to it," came a voice.

Simms squinted through the fog of tobacco smoke and rising steam from fifty or more sodden coats. Men huddled around the bar; others played cards or sat and conversed around tables. In the far corner, a wood burner drew those just arrived. The gabble of raised voices and the clatter of glasses caused everything to be one confused cacophony.

"I said, you'll get used to it."

Simms blinked and turned to the slightly built man at his side. He stood alone, a tumbler of whisky in his hand, a cigar drooping from the corner of his mouth. He wore a black, three-piece suit and a gold watch chain stretched across his midriff from one waistcoat pocket to the next. At his hip, the holster turned inwards for a cross-belly draw, he wore a Colt Navy revolver.

"I'm not planning on staying long."

"I saw you ride in," said the man, tilting the glass. "You ain't no trapper, nor miner either."

Frowning, Simms cast his eyes over the man for a second time. "What's it to you?"

The man shrugged, drawing back his coat to reveal the badge on his chest. "Marshall Nathanial Dixon is who I am. Can I be asking who you might be?"

"I'm the sheriff of Glory, as well as being a Pinkerton stationed over in Bovey."

"A Pinkerton *and* a sheriff. Never heard of such a thing, to share such responsibilities. Why is that, do they not have anyone else suitable for such a position?"

"Maybe, maybe not." Simms, anxious to get away from this interrogation, nodded over to the bar. "I'll get myself a drink. Nice meeting you."

Dixon raised his glass and leaned back against the wall, a wry smile crossing his face.

Simms did not return it.

Some time later, standing in the telegraph office, Simms waited for the operator to check through a communication from Chicago. He handed it to Simms, who read it.

"I've also been asking a few other questions on your behalf," said the operator.

"Oh? Such as?"

"That staging station?" The man checked around the small office, as if half-expecting a figure to appear from out of the shadows. He lowered his voice. "Trent came to see me, so I sent a cable off to Laramie. Seems like it ain't nothing to do with Holladay, the stagecoach boss, or anyone else I've heard of. Some guy called Kieran Danks, out of Kansas City, has set up a stagecoach company to traverse the old Plaite Trail before linking Salt Lake City with other towns and cities across the Territory. So far, all he's done is run a stage from the Kansas border down to Laramie, but his ambitions are far-reaching. This new building project you came across must have something to do with that."

"And O'Shaughnessy? What of him?"

"Well, I got this." He bent down under the counter and produced another communication. He read it aloud, "Liam O'Shaughnessy, wanted throughout the States of Oklahoma and Texas for aggravated burglary, assault and other minor misdemeanours." He looked up. "They are offering a paltry one-hundred-dollar reward for his apprehension."

Simms took the paper and read it himself. Grunting, he gave it back to the man. "A petty thief? Seemed a lot more than that when I met him."

"A gunhand, you mean?"

"That is my guess. Do you know anything about the Marshal I came across, a man called Dixon?"

The man's face blanched and he pushed himself away from the counter. "I do indeed. How do you know him?"

"Met him over in that hole 'Clancy's'. What do you know about him?"

"That he is one hard bastard, that's what. Arrived three days ago and within the hour had pistol-whipped a young guy out in the parade ground. The same day he confronts two swarthy looking Italians over some horse rustling, shoots them both dead. Only then did he present the warrants to the Major. Porter's a flighty individual, more concerned with his lady-friend than anything else, so he didn't question Dixon any further, but people around here were troubled by what happened, saying he acted more like a bounty-hunter than a lawman."

"So why has he stayed, I wonder?"

"Beats me. Maybe he has some unfinished business."

"Yes," said Simms, turning to peer through the open door across the square, his back tingling with developing concern, "my thoughts exactly."

Chapter Seven

Standing on the porch step, the young man in the dark green uniform and pillbox hat flushed with embarrassment as Melody Milligan opened the door to the small house set in a narrow, nondescript street in Kansas City. She giggled at her visitor's shocked expression, well aware of the effect she had on men of all ages. The hand in which he proffered the folded paper trembled.

She gave him a dollar and went back inside to read the telegram. The words made little sense, so she read them again, and by the fourth time of reading, she was giddy with delight. Grabbing her coat and hat, she rushed out of the house and made her way through the busy streets to her good friend Frances, where her boy Tommy was playing with Melody's own son, Patrick.

"I'm not sure what any of this means," said Frances having read the telegram. "A silver strike? What does that mean?"

"What it says. Father has discovered silver. Frances, he's asking me to go."

"Go? To *Colorado*? But, Melody, how can you possibly even consider going all that way? What about Patrick, your job?"

"I'll ask for time off, and Patrick can come with me."

"To Colorado?" Frances's face turned white. "You can't, not *there* – it's wild, Melody. The stories coming out of there chill you to the bone. No, you can't take him." She turned her gaze to the two boys playing together on the carpet, a pile of wooden blocks and lead soldiers surrounding them both as they laughed loudly, oblivious to the two women standing over them. "He can stay with me."

"Stay with you? Frances, no I could never ask you such a thing, I'd—"

"You're not asking, I'm offering. How long will you be? Ten days, a fortnight? I'm sure Jeb and I will cope."

"Are you sure? I mean, it's not as if he's much trouble, but what if—"

"Melody," Frances squeezed her friend's arm, "it'll be fine, but seriously, please think about this. You'll be going into the frontier, with everything that means. And you'll be travelling alone. Please, give it a day or two and think things through. If you're still of a mind to go, then my offer about Patrick stands."

"You're such a good friend," said Melody and leaned forward to kiss Frances on the cheek.

Over the course of the next two days, Melody busied herself with the arrangements. Mr Huntington, her employer at the milliners where she worked, was none too happy when she presented him with the news but agreed to give her two weeks' leave. He didn't have to do that, he insisted, but also added, "Seeing as you are such a diligent young lady, I am willing to grant you a short holiday." She very nearly skipped out of the shop with excitement.

On the second morning after informing Frances, there came another knock on her door and she was surprised to find Nathan Cable, Frances' brother, standing before her, loaded down with a carpet-bag and sporting a finely pressed brown tweed suit. He put down the bag, pulled off his Derby hat and clutched it in front of his midriff, smoothing down his hair before he spoke, "I am pleased to find you at home, Miss Melody."

"Well, it's pleasing to have you call, Nathan. I haven't seen you for some time."

"No, I, er, have only recently returned from a business trip out East."

He shuffled his feet, eyes downcast, uncertain what to say next. Melody relieved the situation by stepping aside and waving him into the hall. "Will you come in and take some tea, Nathan?"

"I will, thank you." He smiled, curling up the brim of his hat in his hands. "Thank you kindly."

"Nathan," she said gently, taking the hat from his clutches, "if you're not careful, you'll bend that poor thing all out of shape."

He cackled and coughed but made no reply. Melody placed the hat on the stand in the hall and motioned him to move into the parlour. Leaving the carpet-bag in the hall, he followed her.

Despite the cold, it was a bright day and a golden glow bathed the little room, making it seem cosy and inviting. He sat on a small sofa, twiddling his thumbs, whilst Melody went out and made the tea.

On her return, she found Nathan sitting in the exact same position and she smiled at that as she poured the tea.

"I shall not take up too much of your time, Miss Melody," he said, taking the tea and staring at it with some puzzlement.

"Drink your tea, Nathan, and relax." She sat down opposite him in the matching armchair beside the fire, which crackled in the grate.

"I do not think I have tasted tea for at least a year." He tried to force a smile, but nothing more than a pained expression was the result. "The last time we met, I believe."

"Yes." She sipped her drink. "I heard you went out East and found yourself a wife."

"Yes, yes, I did. But, as things would transpire, she left me."

"Oh." She stared at him, wide-eyed, expecting more. As the silence continued and it did not appear Nathan was about to elaborate, she smacked her lips and said, "Well, I suppose these things happen."

"Yes. Yes they do." He took a small drink and made a face.

"So, what brings you here, Nathan? You must have heard from Frances that it is my intention to leave for Colorado within the next day or so."

"Yes, she told me, and that is the reason for my visit." He placed his cup on the small table beside the sofa and cleared his throat before continuing. "Frances came to see me, to tell me of your plans. She was very much concerned about your welfare, Miss Melody, so much so that I do not believe I have seen her quite so overcome since the death of our good mother some five years ago."

"Oh my," said Melody, putting down her own cup and pressing her hand to her mouth. "I had no idea. Nathan, what can I say? It leaves me sad and concerned myself that I should be the instigator of—"

"Forgive me, Miss Melody," interjected Nathan, holding up a palm, "do not upset yourself so. All is well. For Frances and I have made a plan, one which we both believe will ease the situation to everyone's benefit."

Frowning, Melody leaned forward. "A plan, Nathan? Whatever do you mean?"

"Yes, Miss Melody. A most admirable plan." He sat up straight, beaming, "I shall accompany you into the Wild Frontier!"

Chapter Eight

From somewhere amongst the trees, an owl hooted and Charlie jumped, breathing hard. Quincy, close by, chuckled. "Jesus, you sure is spooked."

"That's a horrible sound, to be sure," mumbled Charlie, squatting down next to the fence skirting the silent house which loomed ahead of them. The clouds were thick that night, not a star revealed, a fact which would help them to remain unseen. Nevertheless, as Charlie checked the load of his revolver, his hands shook. Mere inches away, Quincy chuckled again. "Let's just get this over and done with."

The two men, crouching low, moved along the fence, separating the house from the path running alongside, searching for a gate. When they could not find one, Quincy slapped his friend hard on the shoulder before hauling himself over, dropping into the manicured lawn on the other side. He scooted across to the rear entrance to the house, trying his best to keep his footfalls quiet on the whitewashed boards of the porch. Turning, he squinted into the darkness, trying to make out Charlie's shape, but could not. Sighing, he moved onto the grass again, whistling softly. "Charlie," he whispered, "where in the name of creation are you?"

"I'm here, you dumb bastard." Charlie's breath sounded ragged and Quincy noticed him rubbing his shinbone. "Got my trouser leg caught, damn it. I think I cut myself."

"Well, when this is all over, you can buy yourself a private nursemaid to look after you."

A flash of white teeth in the darkness. "Wouldn't that beat all?"

"Are you certain this is the right house?"

"Of course I'm certain, Quincy. I watched him leaving the bank when it closed. I'm not a fool."

Quincy grunted and pulled out his gun. "Well, so be it. But come on, the longer we hang about out here, the more likely it is we'll be seen."

"It's three o'clock in the damned morning, Quincy – ain't nobody going to see us."

Without replying, Quincy turned and scurried back to the porch, slowing down as he reached the wooden boards. He crept forward, motioning for Charlie to follow. Then, when he reached the rear entrance, he put his hand around the door handle and turned it.

The door creaked open, horribly loud in the stillness.

Both men froze and waited.

The darkness made it difficult to pick out furniture, or anything else for that matter, and Quincy tried his utmost to move forward with caution. Charlie, however, did not. He blundered into something big and heavy, cursed loudly and fell forward, the object toppling with him. A tremendous smash of pottery shattering followed, a barrage of sound exploding throughout the quiet household.

Quincy dropped to his knees, holding his breath. The sound of Charlie moaning filled the room, but Quincy, unable to make out where his friend was, knelt, trembling, sending out silent prayers that no one had heard the crash. His hopes proved in vain, however, when, with his eyes still unaccustomed to the all-consuming blackness, he spotted a flickering light appearing from somewhere up above. He held his breath.

What followed was swift, frantic and horrible.

A figure appeared, moving down the staircase at the far side of the room. It held an oil lamp aloft, in the other hand a rifle or shotgun of some kind. From where he crouched, Quincy clearly saw the figure's outline. It appeared to be a man and, when the voice came, his suspicions were confirmed. "Whoever you are, you'd better get out now before I blow a hole in you!"

Charlie let out a baleful moan and the man whirled towards it. He put down the lamp and eased back the hammers.

"*Shotgun*," screamed Quincy, diving full stretch to the floor, hands over his ears. The big gun discharged, sending out a wide spread of buckshot, peppering furniture, carpets, walls and anything else in its path. But nothing hit either of the two men. Charlie moaned again, louder this time, and Quincy rose to his feet, picking out the figure in its nightshirt, bathed in the sickly yellow glow of the oil lamp. He fanned his revolver, putting two, three, four slugs into the man's body, blowing him backwards against the stairs. The shotgun slipped from his dead fingers and the body bumped down the stairs until it came to rest at the bottom.

Someone came out from above, screaming. A woman and, behind her, children. All of them setting up such a chorus of cries and screams it seemed to Quincy the whole world would be woken by it. Closing his eyes, he levelled his gun and fired. When the gun was spent, he drew his second revolver and emptied that too. Then he turned and staggered back to the door, vomiting over the porch.

His friend came lumbering up next to him, breath hissing through his teeth. "Jesus, Quincy. You murdered the whole damn lot of 'em."

"Damn you, Charlie! Damn you for doing this."

"*Me*? You're the one who shot 'em all."

"And you were the one who thought this was such a great plan. You never told me he had a wife, and children."

"How in the hell was I to know that? And the plan was to kill him, not everyone! We have to go, goddamnit. We have to go back to camp and make as if we had nothing to do with any of this."

They ran across the lawn, crashing through the fence, no longer caring about the noise they made. Quincy's coat snagged on a broken piece of fencing and he fought desperately to free it.

"Come on, Quincy!"

Charlie loomed forward and seized the coat, yanking it free from the offending piece of splintered wood. The fabric ripped and Quincy, struggling like a thing possessed, freed himself of the garment to leave it hanging there in the cold, night air. Unconcerned, he ran into the nearby woods and the waiting horses. Charlie pounded close behind, but not before taking one, final look back at the house. More lights, from countless oil lamps and candles, danced into the night from the other houses nearby. Soon, the entire town would be awake, roused by the gunfire and the screaming, so Charlie ran, ran faster than he had ever done in his life.

Chapter Nine

Simms slept in the bunkhouse and, in the morning, shivering with the cold, tramped across the square to 'Clancy's' where he took coffee. Bent double over his cup, he pulled a chair up close to the wood-burner, his breath steaming from his mouth. The surroundings were in sharp contrast to how they were when he first arrived. Two hunched soldiers by the counter were the only customers and, by the look of them, they appeared colder than Simms, a fact which he found difficult to accept. He did not think he had ever felt as cold before now and believed he may have caught a chill.

"You look like hell, mister," said the barkeep, his voice booming across the empty room. Simms craned his neck to watch him wiping a spotted rag over the counter top. "You want me to put a whisky in another coffee?"

Simms grunted and managed to smile his thanks as he stood up and shuffled across to the bar. The barkeep tipped a bottle and poured a healthy looking shot of amber liquid into the cup. Simms took a sip and smiled, the coffee tasting even better with the addition of the alcohol.

"Doc Haynes will give you a powder," said one of the soldiers.

Simms studied the rheumy-eyed young soldier, whose stubbled chin dripped with thawing flecks of ice, his nose glowing red. The second fared little better.

"You gentlemen don't appear too good yourselves."

"We just came in from the range. It's damn cold. Seems like the winter has one more string in its tail."

"You with Johnstone's men?" The two soldiers exchanged a look, and Simms added quickly, "I'm a personal friend of the Colonel's. I'm a Pinkerton detective. We've worked together on some cases."

"Well," the first soldier said, "we were detached, ordered to patrol south from the main troop, but then we came upon some trouble. We tried to—"

"Trouble?" Simms flicked his face from one soldier to the other, sensing their unease. "What kind of trouble?"

"We came upon the burnt-out remains of a cabin, or building, or something. Indians must have done it, killing the folk inside and taking the horses."

"I reckon they took the women too," added the second soldier, moving his heavy, rounded shoulders. "Seems that's what them savages is doing more and more these days."

"Are you sure they were Indians?"

The two men bristled and the first, narrowing his eyes, pulled himself up straight. "What do you mean by that? You doubting our word, because if you are—"

"I'm not doubting anything, soldier," said Simms, "but did you find any evidence for it being Indians, is all I'm asking?"

"*Evidence*? Well, who in the name of hell else would it be?"

"There are a lot of dangerous people around, not all of them Natives."

"Dear God," spat the big soldier, "you some sort of Redskin lover? They're murderers and rapists, the whole God damned lot of 'em."

Simms considered his coffee and blew out a long breath. "Some maybe. Just like some whites that do the same."

"Jesus, you really is a Redskin lover – of course it was them! No White man would do such a thing, no sireee."

Nodding, Simms finished his coffee and pushed the empty cup across the counter. The barman was watching him closely, a bemused expression on his florid face. "Where abouts was this?"

"Planning on going out there yourself?"

Simms shrugged and the big one loomed forward and jabbed the detective's shoulder with a thick forefinger, "Planning on checking out if what we say is true?"

"Like you suggest," said Simms, pulling his collar closer to his throat, "I think I might go and pay the good doctor a visit."

"Yeah, well you do that. It'll be a mite safer for you, Mister I'm-a-friend-of-the-Colonel's."

Smiling, Simms doffed his hat and went out.

A flurry of snow whipped around his ankles and soon the cold bit through his clothes and embraced his already frozen flesh. Trembling, he stumbled to the cluster of buildings over to his left, one of which sported a sign announcing it as the office of the army medical officer.

As he stepped up to the door, a group of riders passed through the main doors of the fort. There were four of them, enveloped in huge, thick fur coats. The lead rider wore a Derby hat, a red scarf wrapped around his mouth and jaw, making a useful disguise. His companions were similarly attired and all of them moved slow, their horses suffering like everything else in that hellish place. They reached the livery stable and dismounted and it was then that Simms saw who the lead man was. As he stretched out his back, the man tugged the scarf free from his face and took a deep breath, arching his back to stretch out his cramps.

It was O'Shaughnessy.

Chapter Ten

Leaving the train station, Nathan carried the bags whilst Melody stopped off at a haberdashery to buy more suitable clothes for her forthcoming trek across the frontier. In less than an hour she emerged, dressed in stout black jacket and brown corduroy pants. A floppy, wide-brimmed hat and red neckerchief completed the outfit.

"The man at the store said we really should buy a gun. Or two."

Nathan sucked in his lower lip. "Guns? I never thought of that, Miss Melody."

"Nathan, if we're to be travelling together, I think it's time for you to call me just plain, simple Melody."

"Wow, well ..." He giggled, "Yes, yes that sounds just fine, Miss – I mean, *Melody*."

She laughed as his face flushed red. "Nathan, can you fire a gun?"

"Gosh, me? I don't rightly know. I've never had cause to."

"But you do know about them? That shopkeeper, he seemed mighty insistent."

"He did? Well, I guess I could try one out. Does he sell them?"

"He told me there is a gunsmith, just around the far corner. Maybe we should go."

As things transpired, the gunsmith was two streets down, nestled in between an undertaker's and an import business which, by the display in the window, specialised in silks and cloths from the Far East. Melody pressed her face against the window and cooed. "They look so fine," she said.

"Melody, you want to come on inside this gun shop?"

She laughed and answered without turning, "Oh no, Nathan, I'm more than happy to stay here. Don't be too long."

She heard his footsteps receding, closed her eyes and allowed herself to drift off into a perceived world of stately palaces, heady perfumes and people dressed in the most flamboyant of clothes. Sighing, she wished it was all real but how could she ever know if such places existed, beyond the pages of the books she read? She pressed her forehead against the window and wondered if such things might become reality now that her father was rich.

"I got this," said the small man, stepping out from his backroom, cradling a short rifle, half-wrapped in grey cloth. He laid it down on the counter, untying the restraining string, and pulled the covering away to reveal a fine looking gun.

"It's a Pagent carbine, used by the British cavalry. As you said you would be riding, I thought this would best suit your needs. It's muzzle loading," he continued, pulling down the swivel ramrod, "and this here means you can't lose anything whilst you're reloading from the saddle."

Nathan took the short carbine and sighted down the barrel. "It seems fine," he said, knowing full well he had no idea of the reasons why such a firearm might be termed 'fine'. "Can you show me how to load it?"

After some minutes of instruction, the owner took him to an enclosed rear yard, with sandbags set up against the far wall on the right. "Whilst you take a few shots, what about a nice side arm? Six shots are always better than one, even if the range isn't so good."

"A handgun. Yes, that sounds perfect."

Suitably equipped, Nathan stepped out from the shop, his wallet considerably lighter, but the proud owner of three guns, ample shot, powder and percussion caps. He caught sight of Melody from across the street, waving to him enthusiastically. He took a moment to study her, looking more lovely in her new roughneck clothes than he thought he'd ever seen her. The coat was far too big for her, and the hat covered most of her features, but none of that mattered much to him. Her smile more than made up for anything else.

They took tea in a bustling parlour restaurant, watching the people moving in and out and, through the window, the busy streets. "This doesn't seem like the wild frontier at all," said Melody, biting into a piece of cake. "It's almost like being back home."

"From what I gather, the plains are little more than an hour's ride from here. The man in the gun store said we should follow the trail as best we can and not deviate from it, not one inch."

"That's the old Goldmine trail? The one all them prospectors used to use?"

"And now settlers use it. He said there are lots of settlers setting out across the prairie on a daily basis. He'd never heard of Twin Buttes though."

"Perhaps we should team up with some folk? Might make the journey safer? What do you think?"

"I think anything you say is fine by me, Melody." He smiled and drank his tea. He pulled a face. "Although I'm still not a great lover of this here beverage."

She laughed, reached over and squeezed his hand. "Well, out on the range, we can drink coffee. Like in all the stories I've read."

But Nathan was in no condition to formulate a reply. All of his attention was centred on her hand and the way it pressed into his own. He was grateful he sat, for he felt certain if he were standing, his legs would give way beneath him. So he gulped and smiled, believing himself the luckiest man alive.

Chapter Eleven

Returning to the town of Twin Buttes, they found the place in uproar, with groups of townspeople milling around, all talking at once, faces alive with a mix of fear and anxiety. Tying up their horses outside the saloon, Quincy and Charlie dismounted, doing their utmost to appear intrigued by what they saw. As they stood, a man ran from the newspaper offices clutching a large piece of newsprint which he pinned against the wall of the sheriff's office. People gathered around almost immediately, voices raised, questions asked.

Inside the saloon, the atmosphere was the same. A buzz of conversation filled the small room, men clustered around, many shooting nervous glances towards the two men as they crossed to the bar.

"What's all the commotion, Otis?" asked Quincy, leaning over the counter towards the bartender.

Otis stepped closer, frowning deeply. "Ain't you boys heard?"

"No," said Quincy with a slight chuckle, "that's why I'm asking."

"We been out of town these last few days," put in Charlie.

Otis raised his eyebrows, "Ah, well, in that case … "He glanced towards both ends of the bar, "There's been a killing. Not just your ordinary type either."

"Ordinary type? How can any killing be called 'ordinary', Otis?"

The bartender nodded, "Yes, yes, I know, but *this*. Dear God Almighty, an entire family – massacred."

The two men exchanged a look. "A family?" Charlie shook his head, pointing over Otis's shoulder to the bottles arranged on a shelf. "Two whiskies whilst you tell us all the details."

So, after pouring the drinks, Otis did so, relaying every graphic detail and the two men listened, agog, without muttering a single word.

Later, having downed three measures of whisky each, they sauntered across the street to the assayer's office. Charlie waited outside whilst Quincy entered with a view to filling out a claim form.

Doing his best not to seem too interested, Charlie stood, whistling tunelessly, as people continued to gather, desperate to read the news on the poster. At one point, the sheriff came out of his office, looking tired, his eyes black rimmed and hair tussled.

"There's no point in standing around," he said, hands on hips, shirt hanging out of his trousers. "I've been up all night trying to figure this out and as soon as I—"

"We should muster up a posse, hunts them sonsofbitches down!"

"String 'em up, sheriff. Dear God, ain't there no justice in this world no more?"

"And those children – dear God Almighty, what about those poor children!"

The sheriff brought up his hands, palms outstretched towards the gathering, "Listen, there ain't no point in doing any of those things – we don't even know who the killer is! I sent for a U.S. Marshal to help with the investigation, so we just need to sit and wait."

"Sit and wait?" screeched one astounded woman, "Is that the best you can do? None of us are safe until this maniac is found, Silas. *None of us!*"

The remainder of the crowd took up this point, shouting, brandishing fists, pushing and shoving until it seemed they would storm forward as one and attack. Silas took an involuntary step backwards, one hand falling to the revolver at his hip. "Now you just hold on," he shouted above the increasingly ugly crowd, "I'm doing all I can, but until the Marshal gets here, I need to take this nice and slow. There is no point in blaming me – at the moment, we have not one shred of evidence that will lead us to whoever this murdering bastard is. But, you take it from me, as soon as we find him – and find him we will – his trial will be short and swift."

This did little to convince any of those gathered around and Silas threw his hands up in despair and retreated into his office, slamming the door loudly behind him.

Charlie leaned against a hitching rail, arms folded, chewing frantically at his lips, uncertain what to do next. The crowd continued standing outside the sheriff's and it was some time before they split up, heads down, faces red. Only when they had all drifted away did he cross the street to read the notice.

Schooling was not something Charlie had ever taken seriously. His reading abilities were poor, but even so, he understood the gist.

"Terrible thing."

Charlie whirled around, taken by surprise at the silent approach of the stranger now standing before him. A tall man with a grey, pin-striped frockcoat covering his broad, well-proportioned frame. His face, partly shielded by the brim of his high-crowned black hat, was bent down as his fingers rolled a cigarette. After he popped it into his mouth, lit it and drew the first lungful of smoke, he raised his head and grinned.

Charlie gasped, all of his attention taken by the livid red scar which ran from the corner of the man's left eye to the corner of his mouth. When he spoke, the scar seemed to glow and undulate between purple and blue and back to red again. "Them people. Wonder who'd kill 'em that way. Every single one."

Charlie shook his head, unable to avert his attention from the scar. "Beats me."

Another pull on his cigarette. "I'm here looking for an old friend of mine, wondered if you might know him and where I might find him?"

The man smiled, not a friendly, warm smile, more the smile of someone who expects an answer which may not be to his liking.

"And what might his name be?"

Charlie waited. A movement caught his eye and he looked over the stranger's shoulder to see Quincy emerging from the assayer's office, waving a wad of papers. He stepped down into the street, reading as he came. Charlie turned his eyes to hold the stranger's.

"His name is Dan. Dan Stoakes."

Chapter Twelve

Bending over the bed, the medical officer, holding Simms's wrist, pursed his lips. "It's either a chest infection or, more than likely, a touch of pneumonia."

Simms, looking up into the man's concerned face, groaned. "Ah shit. Pneumonia?"

The medical officer nodded. "My advice is rest, keep yourself warm and eat hot broth. And drink. Water. Lots of it." He turned and summoned the woman standing in the corner to come closer. She was small, wearing a one-piece dark blue quilted robe, covered by a white pinafore. A face, dominated by huge, brown eyes, which told of years of outdoor living, was the colour of teak, her teeth brilliant white as she smiled. "You sure you don't mind looking after him, White Dove?"

Shaking her head, she came up beside the officer and pressed her hand upon the detective's brow. "I shall sit with him."

"Well then, I'll go and fill out my report and pass it on to the Captain." He looked again at Simms. "Just rest, you understand." Then he clipped his medical bag together and left.

Simms turned to the woman as she pulled up a chair and sat down. "How the hell did I get here?"

"You passed out in the square. Some soldiers took you to the bunkhouse, but then the doctor, he said you should come here."

Swivelling his head around, trying to identify something, anything, which might be familiar, Simms muttered, "But where am I?"

"This is Colonel Johnstone's quarters. The doctor, he say that the Colonel would want you here. You are his friend, yes?"

"Yes, yes I am." A bout of violent coughing seized him and he turned over onto his side, doubling up as his body heaved and writhed.

White Dove held onto him, rubbing his back, waiting for the seizure to subside. "Try not to speak anymore. Try to sleep. I will stay."

And Simms, fist clamped over his mouth, forcing air into his lungs, wanted to thank her but the words refused to come, the only sound a terrible rasping wheeze as his coughing subsided. Exhausted, he slumped back into the pillows and watched her through bleary, water-filled eyes, drifting away to the far corner of the room. A tiny moment of despair, thinking she was leaving, followed by intense relief as she returned, a piece of brightly coloured material in her hand, and then everything grew dark as he surrendered to sleep.

Over at 'Clancy's', the press of men's bodies crammed into every available space made the air thick with the tang of sweat and alcohol, yet warm and curiously comforting. Dixon eyed the surroundings with distant interest whilst opposite him, hunched over the small round table, O'Shaughnessy slurped up spoonfuls of steaming stew.

"It may be that he will think nothing of it, until he happens to see you wandering around."

O'Shaughnessy peered at Dixon from under his brows. "In that case, I'll stay out of sight."

"Might be for the best. As a detective, he's bound to do detecting."

"A detective? What in the hell is one of them?" He slurped another helping stew into his mouth, munching down on a particularly difficult piece of meat.

"Says he's a Pinkerton."

"That don't tell me nothin'."

"They're an outfit from out east. Chicago, so I understand."

"Chicago? Jeez, he's a long way from home."

"You ever been to Chicago?"

"Nope. Should I?"

Dixon shrugged, leaning back in his chair. "The Pinkerton Detective Agency is what it's called, and its headquarters are in Chicago. Apparently they are well connected with the government."

"Well, that ain't no recommendation, now is it?"

Dixon laughed and so did O'Shaughnessy, running a piece of bread around the inside of the bowl as he came to the end of his meal. "He'll put two and two together, my friend, no doubt about it."

"Well, in that case," O'Shaughnessy said, dragging his sleeve across his mouth, "I'd best keep him quiet. He's sick you say?"

"So I gather. Pneumonia is what he has. He'll be laid up for a week or so, I shouldn't wonder."

"So," the big man belched, pushing his finished bowl away and grinning through chipped, blackened teeth, "I'll have plenty of opportunity."

"It may not be the best course. Killing a lawman such as him, in a place like this." Dixon shook his head. "I would advise against it."

O'Shaughnessy narrowed his eyes. "You wouldn't be going all soft on me, would you?"

"Do I look like I'm going soft?"

"Nope, but you seem a tad reluctant to do what's right."

"It's not that. The man is a personal friend of Johnstone's. It wouldn't take him long to figure what has happened. There'd be witnesses. He has a squaw nursing him, night and day."

"I'll kill her too. One less Indian in this world has to be a good thing."

"No. You won't kill either of them. For all we know, nature might take its course and he'll die anyway."

"And if he doesn't?"

Dixon blew out his cheeks. "Like I said, you lay low. Simms won't be here forever, even if he does live. My thinking is he'll leave as soon as he is able. I doubt he'll even remember about the stage burning down. No one else will."

"And Danks?"

"Once he hears about the fire, he'll come down." Dixon's unblinking eyes held O'Shaughnessy's. "Then I'll kill him."

"Seems like it's one rule for you, another for everyone else."

"No. What you propose is bound to fail. I'll kill Danks out on the Trail and, just like you did with the fire, make it out to be Indians. No one will link me to any of it."

"Excepting you is his partner."

"And not forgetting that, as a partner, he wrote me out of twenty percent of the profits. The man's a greedy son of a bitch and he'll die for what he did to me."

O'Shaughnessy nodded. "Well, just so long as I get paid, I couldn't give a good damn what you do. But if that Simms fella sees me …" He grinned and winked.

No other explanation was needed.

Chapter Thirteen

In the town of Twin Buttes all seemed quiet, the townsfolk dispersed, the streets deserted. Looking through the front window, absently cleaning a wine glass, Tabatha wondered if she needed to move on. A little under a month before, she came into town on the back of an old mule, her horse having died under her as she pushed the poor animal too hard in the snow. She found the mule at the first ranch she came to. No one else milled about. Most folk were either dead, or had moved back east, the frontier too tough for them. At least, that's how she liked to think of it. As she tramped across the prairie, she did not think much of the people she came across. None of them could compare with her mother and Lamont. Both were dead, and she held Simms entirely responsible. When the time was ripe, and she knew for sure the trail had grown cold, she would backtrack to Glory and put a bullet in the bastard's head.

A voice snapped her out of her reverie. "Anything exciting happening out there, sweetheart?"

Tabatha turned, forcing what she hoped was an apologetic smile. "No, Mrs. Whistler, just wondering where everyone is."

Mrs. Whistler grunted, striding up to her and pulling back the net curtains to get a better view. "Let's hope they all reappear by dinner time. The killing has spooked everyone. I reckon takings will be down for a few nights."

"Or until the sheriff finds 'em."

"Bah, the *sheriff*? He couldn't find a piece of coal in a mine, that one."

"Why was he voted in, then?"

"Because there weren't no one else, that's why. Mr Whistler wanted to do it, and he would have too, if I hadn't dissuaded him." She shook her head, "Nah, I can't see anybody coming in here for dinner tonight."

She stepped away and paused to run her fingers under the rim of the nearest table. "You need to give all of these tables a once-over, Tabatha. This is not your night off."

"No, Mrs. Whistler." Tabatha bit her tongue, watching her employer waddle out of the room through a rear door to the kitchen beyond.

'Ritter's Steak and Chop House' was the first establishment she enquired after a job, and she had no need to look any further. Mrs. Whistler gave her a night's trial and seemed well pleased with the quality of her service.

"Why is it Ritter's and not Whistler's?" she asked her new boss as she stood in the kitchen, polishing the cutlery.

"That's what it was when we bought it," Mrs. Whistler explained. "Old man Ritter died and it was put up for sale." She chuckled, "He died right there." Tabatha recalled the way Mrs. Whistler waggled his finger towards the bottom of the swing door, which opened out into the restaurant. "Half-in, half-out he was, full tray of food in his hands. From what I hear, people were more concerned about the food than they were about him."

She smiled at the memory.

From beyond the window came the loud snort of an approaching horse. She looked out and saw him, a tall man, straight-backed, hat rammed down hard, scarf and thick coat worn to keep out the worst of the cold. The horse, a gray mare, seemed fresh, eyes revealing a keen intelligence. Tabatha liked the look of what she saw.

Leaving the tables for now, she pulled open the door and stepped out, wincing at the cold, icy wind blasting across the wide street. The man, who may or may not have been planning on stopping, pulled on the reins and regarded her with some interest.

"We have good food; it's hot and it's fresh."

Without a word, the man dismounted and tied up the reins at the hitching rail. He doffed his hat and stepped up beside her. She strained her neck to look up into his face, not believing she'd ever met anyone quite so tall.

"I do declare, I am hungry."

"Then step inside. You'll find our welcome as homely as our food."

He chuckled. "That's an invitation hard to resist."

She gave him her best coy smile. "I hope so."

He paused before motioning to his horse. "I'll need to stable Mary before I do anything else."

"Nice name for a horse."

"She's given me loyal service over the years and I love her dearly."

"You *love* her?"

He frowned at her startled expression. "Of course. We've been through some bad scrapes and she's never let me down. You could say I owe her my life."

She stared without speaking for a few moments, then said, "I'll send Oliver, our kitchen porter."

He dipped into one of his pockets and brought out a silver dollar coin. "This should cover it, and his time."

She took the coin and studied it for a moment. "Ain't seen one of these for a while."

"Well, you have now. Can we get in out of the cold? I've been on the trail longer than I care to think about."

She stepped aside and, almost filling the door space, he went inside.

"Who's this?"

It was Mrs. Whistler, her aggravating sixth-sense once again serving her well. She stood with her arms folded, head tilted, mouth a thin line, curiosity mingled with suspicion.

"Name is Dodd," said the man, taking off his hat and removing his scarf.

Mrs. Whistler's eyes widened as she took in him in, allowing her gaze to linger on his broad shoulders, grizzled chin and those piercing blue eyes, which returned her own stare with a hint of amusement.

"We're not a boarding house," she snapped, her cheeks reddening and she blustered out of the room.

Dodd turned to Tabatha. "Firebrand, huh."

"Her bite is much worse than her bark," she added, with a smile. She stepped forward, "Let me take your coat."

Nodding his thanks, he allowed her to fulfil her suggestion and then settled down at a table. "Quiet."

"It's the killing," she said, hanging the man's coat and hat on the stand in the corner.

"Killing?"

"Yes," she returned to the table, producing a tiny notepad from the front pocket of her pinafore. "A whole family, murdered. Nobody knows why, or who it was."

"Yes, that'll be the poster I saw everyone gathering around. Terrible thing it must have been – a whole family? Dear God."

"The town is in shock and no one is daring to venture out, so," she waved her arm around in a wide arc, "the place is your very own."

"Well, in that case, I shall have the best you can offer."

"I'll see to it," she said, without writing anything down and went to move away.

"A boarding house? Is there one?"

"No, not as such. There was a hotel once, but it closed down. You might find a room over at the saloon."

"And where do you stay?"

She went to speak but stopped herself, picking up on the playful glint in his eyes. So she gasped, put her hand to her mouth and whirled away, feeling the heat rising to her cheeks.

As she went into the kitchen she heard his low, gentle, mocking laugh.

Chapter Fourteen

They set out early the following morning. Nathan had the use of a map, which a travelling salesman, sitting at the next table, handed over to him. "Begging your pardon, but I couldn't help but hear you're about to undertake a journey west." He nodded towards the creased up map. "This'll aid you as you cross the prairie. I won't be having need of it from now on."

Melody, looking up from her breakfast, frowned. "Why is that?"

"Best not for you to ask, little lady." He squeezed Nathan's shoulder. "You just take care," he said mysteriously.

Out on the prairie, they set a steady pace, the town before long becoming little more than a black smudge on the horizon.

"I'm going to miss that place," said Melody, twisting in her saddle to look back. "It's the kind of place I believe I could settle down in."

By the look on Nathan's face, she could tell he did not agree and she laughed. "Give me a broad street, a theatre and a few decent restaurants, Miss Melody. That would be where I'd settle."

"You're an old fuddy-duddy, Nathan. And," she stretched across and gave him a playful jab in the arm, "quit calling me Miss."

With his laughter ringing out through the wide, open plain, thoughts of the little town soon faded and they lapsed into silence, the sound of their horses' hooves plodding across the broken ground ringing through the nearby mountains. They made good progress, neither of them speaking as they took in their surroundings. Following a series of bluffs through which the trail snaked, they passed from fertile pasture to rock-strewn plains, ascending over rocky hilltops and through winding valleys. As the day slipped by, the temperature dropped, forcing them to pull on their thick blanket coats. The sky, endlessly blue and cloudless, promised a cold, perhaps freezing, night ahead.

By early evening, tired and hungry, they found a sheltered area amongst the rocks and made camp. Nathan bent down, using a flint and steel to strike sparks into a mound of dried sage grass and bracken, which soon took light. He fed the tiny flames with more pieces of wood until the flames lapped upwards, growing in intensity.

Meanwhile, Melody broke up pieces of bacon into a pan, licking her lips with expectation. "This ain't so bad," she said, laughter tingeing the edge of her words. "When I was little, my pa would often take us out on little trips into the mountains. We'd camp out under the stars ..." Her voice trailed away and she sighed. "I hope we find him well, Nathan."

"I'm sure we will," said Nathan, moving around sticks and twigs, keeping the fire going. "But you're right, this is nothing like what that salesman was warning us about. Take care? Take care about what?"

"Wolves maybe. Coyotes. I hear they can be dangerous when hungry."

"Yeah, but the fire will keep 'em away. I'll make sure I stack it up nice and big before we sleep."

Whistling a half-forgotten tune, she moved across to the fire and settled the pan on top. Within seconds, the bacon sizzled and spat and she used a wooden spoon to turn them. "I have some *tortillas* and a few tomatoes in my saddle bag – this is going to be a feast, Nathan."

He turned to her and his eyes shone with something more than delight. As he moved closer, she cupped his face in her hands. "Oh Nathan. You think we should?"

For a reply, his grin broadened and he turned his head in preparation to kiss her.

Later they lay close under their blankets, shivering in the cold despite the close proximity of the fire.

"I don't think I've ever felt so frozen," she said, her voice sounding small in the dark. He kissed her and held her and soon sleep enveloped them both.

In the morning, she cooked a breakfast of ham and leftover tortillas. Munching through their meal, both sat and looked out across the vastness of the land before them. "There's a river out there," said Nathan, studying their route, tracing a greasy finger across the threading blue line bisecting the map. "It'll be a good place to rest the horses, and perhaps we'll meet up with some other folk travelling west. I heard it said that once, not so many years ago, there were hundreds, if not thousands, of pilgrims passing this way."

"That was the promise of gold, so I understand. California offered a new beginning for so many."

"And your pa. He must have come this way?"

Her eyes grew distant. "Well, he's struck it rich now, Nathan. And he didn't need to reach California to do so."

"All being well, we should reach Twin Buttes in two or three days." He reached over and squeezed her hand. "Then we can have something of a celebration."

Smiling, she leaned into him and he held her, kissed the top of her head and sighed. His hand dropped to her breast and she moaned. They made love again, in the sharp, clean air of the morning and afterwards lay for a long time, staring at the sky.

Some hours later, they followed the trail across the plain, as so many had done before them, travelling towards the promise of a new life. Through a valley flanked by towering rocks, they descended slowly into a broad flat plain, open and vast, and at one point Nathan reined in his horse to look out towards the horizon and a line of rolling hills. Not noticing, Melody continued for a few more paces before she stopped and turned to frown back at him. "What is it?"

"I thought I saw riders, but they dropped out of sight."

"Could be anyone. Maybe some of those pilgrims you spoke about."

"Could be." Nathan stretched himself in the saddle. "We'll make the river by sundown, so we'll know for sure then."

But at the river, they found nothing but an abandoned, broken wagon and the signs of an old camp, pieces of rusted equipment scattered here and there and, most bewilderingly, a single black leather boot.

"Soldiers," he said to himself as he bent down to study the abandoned footwear. "Wonder why they left the wagon?"

"Looks like it's been here for some time," she said, leading the horses through the lush grass to the edge of the river. Gently flowing, the bed visible through the clear, shallow water, she allowed the horses to drink whilst she stooped and filled up her canteens. On the far side, the trees skirted the bank and somewhere a bird sang its plaintive song. "It's so beautiful," she said in whispered awe.

"It won't be as cold here tonight," said Nathan, throwing down their bed rolls, "but I'll still make a fire. There may be bears in that wood."

"Bears? You think so?"

He shrugged, patting his holstered revolver, "We're well protected, Melody."

"I hope you know how to use that thing, Nathan."

"It can't be that difficult. You just pull it, aim it and shoot." Laughing, he followed his own instructions, drawing the gun and aiming it at the thick spread of trees. He eased back the hammer but paused in the act of firing a bullet. "Best not frighten anything that might be lurking in there."

Melody shivered and stepped back from the river's edge, pushing down the cork stoppers of her canteens. "Don't talk that way, Nathan, it gives me the jitters. Perhaps we should find some high ground, amongst the rocks."

"Don't you worry none," he said, holstering the gun and running his arms around her waist.

She smiled as she turned in his arms. "I won't worry with you here," she said, peering up into his face.

Sometime in the night, she sat up, senses alert, staring out into the blackness. Groaning beside her, Nathan propped himself with one arm, yawning. "What is it?"

"I don't know," she said, rigid, straining to hear. "I thought I heard something."

Rubbing his eyes, he sat up next to her. "I'll go check."

As he went to stand, she caught hold of his shirttails. "Be careful."

Chuckling, he took up his revolver. "I'll go check the horses first."

She watched him disappearing into the gloom and waited. Beyond her, the river trickled by, the only sound in that gentle place, and slowly her shoulders relaxed and her breathing eased. Whatever it was that woke her, it was surely nothing dangerous. A rabbit, or some other tiny animal moving through the grass, nothing to be afraid of or bring her—

Nathan came crashing towards her, stumbling through the grass, gasping and he dropped down to his knees, the whites of his eyes glaring in the darkness.

"Oh sweet Jesus," he said.

She held onto his face, squeezing his cheeks, feeling his body trembling. "What in the name of God is it?"

"The horses," he said, his voice full of disbelief, "they've gone."

They waited until morning, neither of them wanting to eat, and they searched for their animals in the pale light.

"I hobbled and tied them down real well," said Nathan, standing in his shirt, contemptuous of the chill, the expression on his drawn face revealing the despair he felt.

"What are we to do?"

He turned to her, lips trembling. "They must have been taken."

"*Taken*? But who—"

He went to take a step towards her. The arrow hit him in the nape of the neck and, for a single moment, they both stared into one another's eyes in disbelief. Then the light went out of his eyes, he pitched forward and Melody screamed.

They came out of the chilly morning air, like demons from the bowels of hell, their mouths opened in high-pitched screams, hatchets raised in their hands, falling upon the couple in a thick swarm. Overpowered, terrified, confused, Melody tried to scurry away, but there were too many and they cut off any possibility of escape. She whirled, not daring to believe any of it was happening, but then they closed in around her, cackling and drooling, teeth bared, a pack of hungry dogs. Desperate, she tried to fight them, flailing away with her tiny fists, but they overpowered her with ease. They were strong, wild and determined. Two of them held her and, as she struggled in their powerful grips, she watched in horror as two others hacked at Nathan's head, chopping off the scalp, raising it, dripping with blood, to show their new trophy.

"Oh sweet Jesus," she gasped as other hands ripped away her clothing and the closest brave moved towards her, tongue hanging out, mouth slack with desire, groping at his pants to release himself.

A sharp command stopped everyone. The warriors parted, making way for the man striding towards them, his torso bare and rippling with muscle. Melody looked at him. The man's eyes, burning with barely contained rage, lingered on her as he barked out further commands in a strange, guttural language. The others moved away, crestfallen.

He reached out his hand, seized hers and pulled her to her feet. His voice sounded gentle when he next spoke but, as she could not understand, she merely shrugged and shook her head. Then, in a swift movement, he had her around the waist and lifted her over his shoulder. She had no more strength to resist and as he took her away, she caught sight of what remained of Nathan and her tears burst out unchecked.

Thrown over the back of a pony, someone lashed her wrists together. She was now their prisoner and, overwhelmed at this awful truth, she slipped into a dead faint.

Chapter Fifteen

Simms chuckled to himself, noting his hand did not shake as he brought the spoon to his mouth. Hovering close by, a look of quiet satisfaction crossed White Dove's face. "You will soon be able to go outside again," she said.

He grunted, slurping up the steaming broth. He licked his lips. "This is good."

Another smile and she left the room. He listened to her moving about beyond the door and wondered why she nursed him the way she did. For two nights, she sat next to his bed, wiping his brow, holding his hand, sometimes bathing him with a cold cloth, other times wrapping the blankets close about him as he drifted in and out of his fever. She rarely spoke, sometimes hummed an unknown tune, an old Indian one perhaps. Thoughts of who she was, where she came from, what tribe she belonged to crossed his mind. Her face, a deep brown colour, was finely chiselled, her eyes penetrating and huge, her lips full, jaw line strong. Whenever she touched him, a thrill ran through his body, her fingers so gentle, so assured. The longer she remained in his company, the more he yearned for her presence and every time she slipped away, a cold emptiness enveloped him.

Later that same day, he pulled back the covers and clambered out of bed. Crossing the small room, he looked out through the window and into the square. Quiet, with few people about, he noted how white the sky was. Snow would fall soon. Winter's grip was not yet weakened and he groaned at the thought. He longed for spring, the warmth of the sun a distant memory.

Unaware of her approach until he slipped up alongside him, he gave a little jump, then laughed at her upturned face and her smile.

"I am pleased you are stronger."

Before he knew what happened, his arms were around her waist, their lips melting into each other's. His body, weakened by the sickness, did the best it could, but, very soon, White Dove took the lead, taking him to the bed, hands and lips seeking out his urgent need, moving over him, making love to him in a way he had never known nor even believed possible.

Afterwards they lay entwined within the sheets, her fingers gently caressing his brow until sleep conquered him and, contented, warm, all of his fears banished, he slipped into a world of dreams, none of them bad.

She found him packing his things into two saddlebags. Unaware of her presence, he carefully checked the load of his guns, aiming along the barrel of the pocket Colt before fitting it carefully into its holster strapped to his calf.

"You always carry that one?"

He gave a little start, then grinned. "I'm going to have to be careful with you around – I can never hear you coming up behind me."

Shrugging, she moved into his open arms and he held her close. "You are leaving?"

"I have to get back to Bovey – they'll be wondering where I am."

She sighed, pressing the side of her face into his chest. "I am thinking, perhaps I could come with you?"

Her face came up, expectantly, and they held one another's gaze.

"You have to know something. Not all white folk are like me. They are suspicious of Native people; some would not welcome you." He placed his hands on her shoulders, holding her at arm's length. "But you could live in my ranch. It's not big, not by any means. I have a few horses, always thought of keeping more."

"I am good with horses."

"I thought you might be." He smiled. "So long as you understand, people in town, they might—"

"I will not go into town. I shall stay at the ranch, tend to the horses."

"That's music to my ears." He pulled her to him again and kissed the top of her head.

"It is strange you do not have a woman."

She felt his body tense and she waited, holding her breath, not daring to think what his answer might be.

"I did have," he said at last. "She died giving birth to our child."

After a respectful silence, she said simply, "I am sorry."

She helped him prepare for the journey, fetching his horse from the livery stable, ignoring the sideways glances from the soldiers as she strode purposefully across the square.

"Hey, brown eyes," shouted a burly, sour-faced soldier leaning against a hitching rail, smoking a foul-smelling cigar, "where is you off in such a hurry?"

White Dove ignored him, but on reaching the Colonel's quarters, another soldier stood, barring her way. Younger than the other one and not as big, his face revealed a far more sinister nature. Where the other could be termed a wolf, this one was surely a weasel.

"I been meaning to come call on you, pretty one," he said, the leer across his mouth telling her everything she needed to know. He stood on the slightly raised walkway, in front of the door, legs planted apart, jaw jutting forward, arrogance visible in every move he made, every word he spoke.

She stepped up to him, unperturbed. "Get out of my way, soldier."

His face broke into an expression of exaggerated shock, "Ooh my, pretty one, don't you frighten me none."

"I will do more than that if you do not move."

He pursed his lips, his hands coming up, fingers wriggling, "I'm scared."

She swung her foot between his legs, slamming the kick into his groin. He yelped, the air rushing out of his mouth. Bending double, face growing purple as he clutched at his nether regions, he crumpled to his knees, moaning loudly.

White Dove went to move, but his companion, the big one, had her around the midriff and was whirling her around. She struggled, kicking and punching, screeching loudly, but all to no avail. His strength was too much and he flung her down into the dirt, hard. "You dirty little bitch," he roared, reaching for his waistband. As he unbuckled his belt, she scurried backwards across the ground, eyes alive with fear.

"I'm gonna teach you a goddamned lesson, you heathen whore."

The door creaked open and White Dove looked past the big soldier's shoulders to see Simms standing there.

"Try that on me, soldier boy."

She saw it, but never knew such a thing could happen. The big man, like a bull, swinging a great punch, and Simms ducking low to strike him in the stomach, then the jaw, then again in the face, punches so fast, so hard, they seemed as one. The big man swayed but did not go down, so Simms drove on, another right, then a left to the guts and another to the jaw. The soldier was teetering on legs turned to liquid. They could not hold him and he dropped. Simms kicked him across the side of the head and he flew alongside her, hitting the ground with a sickening crunch.

She stared at the blood drooling from the big soldier's broken mouth and then Simms was beside her, helping to her feet. His eyes, so full of concern, holding her, cradling her head as if she were a child.

And then the first soldier reared up, his hand going for the revolver at his belt.

"You wanna die, boy, you just go right ahead and pull that gun."

Simms held her, looking at the soldier over his shoulder and she saw the soldier taking in the big Colt Dragoon which had materialised in Simms' hand. Something flickered in the soldier's eyes, an uncertainty, all his former arrogance gone, replaced by something else – fear. "I'll kill you, you bastard."

"You can try," said Simms evenly and she wondered if he would have time to release her, turn and bring up his gun. She did not know, and neither did the soldier. Common sense prevailed. His body relaxed and he sniffed loudly, pressing the back of his hand against his nose, other hand swinging free. He stepped down and went to his friend. Then his eyes locked on White Dove and they hardened. "You too. I'll kill you both."

Simms took her into Johnstone's quarters and closed the door behind them.

She stood, looking at him and when her lips parted to speak, he held up his hand. "I know, and I'm sorry, but it's what I do."

"I did not, I would not ... " She averted her eyes. "I know so little about you."

"I'm a lawman, and that means I have to do things others might find distasteful. It's not something I enjoy."

"I understand."

"Do you?" He moved up to her, his face changed. Gone the loving, kind, caring man who held her so close and who groaned so loud as she touched him. Instead, here was someone different. Meaner, harder. Dangerous. "I've killed people, White Dove. More than once. I served in the war against Mexico back in Forty-Seven. I learned how to kill back then. The things I did, I ain't proud of. And since then, since becoming a Pinkerton, I've been forced to do it again and again. Natives too. You need to know that if you're to be with me."

"Your woman knew all of this?"

"Some. I saved her from a bunch of Utes who raped her and would have killed her." He closed his eyes for a moment. "There were four of them, and I shot them all dead. Noreen and I, we had that between us. An understanding. A truth."

"Well," she said, trying to stop her voice of trembling, "I have the truth also." She went over to his saddlebags, picked them up and looked at him, unblinking. "And now, I think we should go."

From his seat near the window of 'Clancy's', Dixon pulled hard on his cheroot before blowing out a long stream of smoke. He swivelled around and peered through the swirling mist of smoke and stale sweat to pick out O'Shaughnessy, standing at the counter in deep conversation with a much smaller man. "Come and see this," shouted the marshal.

After saying a few parting words, O'Shaughnessy swaggered over, glass in hand, and frowned. "What?"

Dixon motioned to the square on the other side of the misted up window. The marshal had rubbed a vision hole in the grime and condensation. "Your friend seems a lot better."

A loud sigh and O'Shaughnessy leaned to the glass, pressing his nose up against the cold pane. "What is it I'm looking at?"

"See the big guy on the ground?" O'Shaughnessy grunted. "Simms just beat the living shit out of him."

"So?"

"See the other guy, kneeling down next to his unconscious pal?"

"I do. Is Simms gonna beat him up too?"

"Nope. Simms has returned indoors with his lady-squaw. I reckon he's planning on leaving. Saw her heading up to the door with saddlebags and bedrolls, before the big guy tried it on with her. That's when Simms stepped in."

"He's leavin'? Where's he headin'?"

Dixon shrugged. "How am I supposed to know that? Thing is, if he leaves, we have no way of knowing which way he'll head. My guess is, he'll pass by what remains of the staging station. When he reaches his town, he may even receive some words from our mutual acquaintance, Danks."

O'Shaughnessy scowled, leaning back from the glass. "You really think Simms will have even a single idea about what happened?"

"He's a detective, so I'm sure he'll soon be able to decipher that no Indians burned the place down. That'll leave Danks with only one conclusion – it was me. He'll send a goddamned army over here to flush me out." He drew on the cheroot. "I can't allow that to happen. I've been thinking long and hard about it and I've changed my mind. I need that bastard detective dead, so I can get what is mine."

"So you want me to kill Simms right now, is that it?"

"No, not Simms."

"Jesus, the squaw? Dixon, I am many things but I ain't no—"

"Not the squaw – the soldier kneeling there, caring for his pal."

O'Shaughnessy's frown grew deeper. "How is that gonna help?"

"Because you take him down a back alley and shoot him in the back of the head. Then, you and some of you partners," he pointed with his cheroot towards the bar, "you swear you saw Simms following our good ol' soldier-boy and, the next thing you know, there is shootin'. There can be only one conclusion to draw from it."

"Simms will take the fall ... Jeez, you think it'll work?"

Dixon beamed and leaned back in his chair, arms crossed, cigar glowing, "Oh yes, I sincerely do."

Chapter Sixteen

Encroaching walls pressing in, black, formless, the sharp tang of sweat and rawhide invading nostrils; everything confused, warped, a world of despair. Melody rolled over, groaning, her eyes growing accustomed to the dimly lit interior. Forcing herself up, pushing down with her palms on the hard, damp earth, blinking, the only sound the pounding of her heart in her ears. She opened her mouth, sucking in a breath, and had to stop herself from screaming.

She wore buckskin clothes, rough against her skin, an unforgiving material, cold to the touch. On her feet, moccasins, around her throat a necklace of bone, possibly horn. She thought of tugging it free but then, as the memory of Nathan and the manner of his death returned, she leaned over and vomited into the dirt, retching loudly, guts and throat straining, bile burning as it left her. Gasping, she fell back against the sides of her prison and looked up to where the sides came together, saw the way the poles or sticks joined at the top. "A tepee," she said and suddenly it all came flooding into her mind and she broke down, despair conquering her.

After draping her across a piebald pony, whooping as they did so, jubilant with their prize, someone smacked the animal's rump and it broke into an uneven canter. Forced awake, she tried to keep her eyes fixed on the ground trailing beneath her, the terrain broken and difficult. Bucking and jarring, she gritted her teeth, eyes travelling across the ground as the hard spine of the pony pressed into her stomach. Fearing she would fall, she clung on, one hand gripping the base of its tail, the other finding a piece of hard flesh to hold on to. She remembered someone slicing through the bonds with a knife. His face looking at her, his voice gentle. The tears stung her eyes, but the ignominy hurt far more.

Arriving at their camp, the Indians dragged her through a tight knit-group of baying women and lusty youths towards a cluster of tepees. Thrown inside, the main warrior stepped in after her. He said something. She shrugged. Without warning, his face contorted into a terrible scowl and he punched her across the jaw, the blow as hard as a stone, sending her senses reeling until blackness enveloped her.

And now, here she was, the ghastliness of it running around inside her head. What to do, where to go. To die, or succumb; there really was no other choice. Nathan was dead, scalped, his body stripped naked and flung over a cliff, food for buzzards and coyotes. Nathan, whose only fault was wanting to help her too much. Perhaps he loved her, perhaps in another world ...

She pressed her face into her hands and wept. She was still crying when the flap opened to reveal the warrior who hit her. A tiny, strangulated yelp of fear came from her constricted throat and she shuffled backwards as he stepped forward and stood over her, eyes alive with desire.

"Wait," she said, bringing up both her hands.

He stopped, a frown creasing his deeply tanned face. A tiny, barely perceptible shake of the head before he took another step.

"I said *wait*, God damn you!"

The warrior recoiled a little, uncertainty crossing his face.

"You touch me again and I'll kill myself. Do you hear me?" His face remained unchanged, nothing very much registering. "Do you understand me? Do you even *know* what I'm saying to you, you devil?" Still the dead look. "Answer me, Goddamn your eyes!"

The tepee flap burst open and a small, powerfully built woman strode in, pushing the young warrior to one side. He shrieked at her but, ignoring him, she dropped to her knees and put her arm around Melody's shoulders. A few words, spat out in short bursts, and the warrior clenched his teeth, grunted a few times, then stomped out like a petulant, chastised child.

Melody, breathless, full of questions, turned in the woman's arms and broke down again. In this stranger's arms, she experienced something she thought had died alongside Nathan – hope.

She must have fallen asleep again, for when she opened her eyes, the woman was gone. She waited, half expecting another attack, a further assault on her body, but when nothing happened, she relaxed and took the chance to sit up. The flap to the tepee was open and, taking a deep breath, she roused herself and crawled through into the daylight.

A cluster of around half a dozen other tepees lay in a rough circle, pitched around a central area where a large fire smouldered. Several naked children played amongst the charred pieces of wood and buffalo droppings, laughing, full of joy. One caught sight of Melody, gestured for the others to look and they all stood, frozen, aghast.

There were women working in various areas of the encampment, some beating at dried skins, others preparing meat, several labouring at sewing together pieces of clothing. A silence fell over every one, eyes taking her in, studying her, and she felt the atmosphere change, growing tense and unwelcoming.

An old man, bent almost double, shuffled across to her. Using an old, twisted stick to support his weight, he painted a curious picture as he struggled in his approach, pausing now and then to cough, hack and spit into the ground. Two paces from her, she saw how creased his face was, a walnut face, ravaged by time, endless years of outside living having chiselled deep furrows in his flesh. Watery eyes studied her, cracked lips parting, words drooling, making no sense.

"Where am I?" she asked, with as much humility as she could muster, fighting down the fear which gnawed away inside.

The man's answer proved as incomprehensible as his first few words and she looked around, desperate to seek out the woman who helped her earlier.

"Why do you seek to know such a thing?"

Melody span around, taken aback by the voice and she blinked, surprised to find a tall, well-muscled man of indeterminate age standing before her, blue-black hair hanging loose to his shoulders. He wore animal skin breeches, exposing the thighs, with a breech-cloth of bright blue in the centre. A necklace made from what looked like claws half covered his sleeveless vest, but she dared not stare at him for too long, for he oozed immense strength and authority. Her eyes dropped to the ground.

He stepped closer, cupping his fingers under her chin to lift her head. She stared into his eyes, mesmerised, finding not only power there but something akin to kindness.

"I know your language," he said, "so speak. Tell me who you are, and why Long Elk brought you here."

"I ... " She wanted to tell him everything, to plead for her release, to ride across the plain and be with her father. To find Nathan. To touch him, feel him so close once more. To wake from this nightmare.

"You must have no fear," he said. "I am The Moon That Rises, and I lead my people here. My father," he nodded to where the old man stood, leaning on his stick, "is old and his days are numbered now, but he is wise and we have spoken of you. Your beauty enthralls our warriors and Long Elk has fought, and will fight again, for your favour."

"My favour?" she said, finding her voice at last, angered by this assumption. "*Favour*? He forced himself upon me."

He dropped his hand, eyes hardening slightly. "You did not fight. You gave yourself willingly."

Another memory loomed large in her mind. His body, pressed over her, rousing her from her faint. Then the terrible knowledge of what was happening. "I was asleep – I fainted. I had no choice."

"Choice? What is that? I know not what such a word means."

"He, this Long Elk, he attacked us. We were no threat, we were simply—"

"Us? Long Elk told of your companion, a man with guns. Long Elk killed this man and claimed you as his trophy. You are his woman now."

"No. I am not."

He loomed over her, and for a moment she believed she had gone too far as she saw the rage burning in his eyes. "You had best learn your place. I see in you a good heart, but your sharp tongue will bring you only suffering, so take care. You are one of us, and we will protect you."

Her breath came in short stabs, laced with disbelief, horror and fear. "One of you?"

"You must work, with the other women, and serve your husband."

Her mouth fell open. "Husband?"

"Long Elk is your man. Forget the other. He was weak and he is dead. His scalp hangs in Long Elk's tepee to remind you that you now have a man of strength, a man of virility."

"But I don't want anything to do with him. Or you." She whirled around, sweeping her arm in a wide arc, "Or any of you. My name is Melody Milligan out of Kansas City, and I'm on my way to meet with my father. Once I get there I will—"

"*No.*" His voice cracked like a whip and she recoiled, hand flying to her mouth, the tears springing from her eyes. "You are *one of us*. Long Elk wishes it to be so, and I have agreed. You will submit, or you will die."

Without another word, he pushed past her, approaching the old man, clamping his hand on his father's shoulder and leading him slowly away. Melody stood and watched and, for the first time in her life, wished she was dead.

Chapter Seventeen

They came not long afterwards, four of them, an officer and three soldiers, all armed. Simms gave White Dove a look and raised his arms, allowing one of the men in blue to relieve him of his weapons. With White Dove's sobs ringing in his ears, he let them escort him across the square to the jailhouse. A crowd gathered outside to watch, silent, anger brewing in every hard stare.

Porter stood inside the jailhouse, drinking steaming hot coffee. From the look of him, the dishevelled hair, the dark rimmed eyes, it seemed to Simms the man had only recently dragged himself out of bed. He wondered who he shared his night with this time.

"Disappointed," the major said, watching the men bringing Simms inside whilst the Lieutenant unlocked the cell door.

Simms stood, shoulders sagging. "Don't suppose there's much point in me asking what the hell this is all about?"

"We have witnesses who saw it all," said Porter in a bored voice, staring into his coffee cup as if he saw something unusual in there. He grunted, hurled the grounds across the floor and glared towards the Pinkerton as beyond him the cell door creaked open on its rusted hinges.

"Saw it all?" Simms looked at each of the soldiers in turn. "Saw all what?"

"You," snapped the lieutenant. "How you argued with two of our men, then followed one of them down a side passage and put a bullet in the back of his head."

Simms gaped.

"You'll answer for it," said Porter. "The witnesses will be called at your trial and justice will be done. Put him inside."

Bundled into the cramped confines of the cell, Simms stood and glared back at the major. "It's true I beat those two ingrates down, but I didn't kill either of them."

"Denial is futile," said the lieutenant.

"Ah yes, of course, you have witnesses. Strange that," said Simms, voice flat, betraying no trace of emotion, "as when it happened, the entire square was empty."

"Well, you got that wrong," said Porter stepping up close to the iron bars. "You killed one of my boys, put the other in hospital. You're going to pay."

Simms realised at that point the enormity of his situation. He felt his stomach lurch and, for a moment, the shockwave screaming through him prevented him from speaking. He swallowed hard. "Look, just tell me what in the name of God you are talking about?"

"Don't try and deny it, you piece of scum – there were people there. They saw you walk up behind that poor boy and shoot him dead. In the back, you miserable bastard."

"Listen, if I did put one of them in the hospital, that's because he swung at me first. But the other, I didn't touch him. He was about to go for his gun and I—"

"If you want my opinion," said Porter, sucking at his teeth, "I wish to God he had gone for his gun and saved us all a whole lot of bother. You spend three days in the commander's quarters, treating it like some goddamned hotel, plus you take up with that squaw, which is beyond reason and, I should think, against the law."

"That's bullshit, all of this is *bullshit* – and you know it."

Porter's hands came up, bunched into fists. "You arrogant sonofabitch. We're going to put you on trial and hang you, but not before we dispense some of our own, personal justice."

He stepped aside and Simms watched as the other soldiers took off their uniform jackets and slowly rolled up their shirt-sleeves.

"It'll take more than three of you," said Simms, shuffling his feet in the ground, changing his stance.

Porter nodded, grinning. "Not if we have some help," he said, pointing into the corner where there were stacked a bunch of what looked like pickaxe handles. Chuckling amongst themselves, the soldiers picked up their chosen implements and, weighing them in their hands, moved as one towards the cell door.

"Open it, Lieutenant."

The young officer seemed uncertain, sucking in his bottom lip, eyes flickering this way and that. "Sir, I'm not sure this is the right thing to do. Maybe we should wait for the Colonel before we—"

"That's an order, boy," snarled Porter.

But the Major's words made little impression on the young officer, who continued to prevaricate, the colour draining from his face. Losing patience, Porter reached over and snatched the bunch of keys from the lieutenant's hands. He fitted the key in the lock, "Best get outside, boy, if you can't stand what's about to happen." Porter turned the lock and stepped back, grinning. "Me, I'm gonna watch the show."

She went visiting Simms at the jail and when she saw him, lying in a heap in the corner of his cell, with an old, threadbare blanket thrown over him, she thought she would pass out. Emitting a tiny wail, she held onto the door-jamb, unable to focus as the tears sprang from her eyes.

"He ain't so bad," drawled the big, burly soldier on the other side of a desk strewn with every piece of rubbish, torn papers, spilt drink, scraps of food, all of it stinking and filthy. He pushed himself to his feet by his palms and leered, "So don't you go worrying your pretty little head none. Besides," he came around the desk, his great bulk straining the buttons of his shirt, "if it's company you're needing..."

He loomed up close. White Dove turned her head away, recoiling as the foul smell of his whisky-sodden breath wafted over her. "Please, I just want to make sure he is all right."

"He's fine," said the soldier, brushing up closer still, one podgy hand running through her braided hair. "My, you are a sweet young thing. Would you like a drink?"

White Dove shook her head. The soldier, unable to keep the disappointment out of his voice, or his expression, swayed back to his desk, "Suit yourself," he said, rifling through the drawers until he found a bottle and brandished it. "Fine, eight-year-old Bourbon, the best there is." He clattered the neck of the bottle into a dirty glass and drained it in one. "You can't talk to him," and he belched and flopped back into his chair.

"But I—"

"I told you," he said, pointing a thick finger at her, "he's *compus* whatever-you-call-it, somesuch fancy word the Lieutenant used. Either way, he's out of bounds. Call back tomorrow, he might be awake and you can send him some kisses." He giggled and titled the bottle.

"You will be here tomorrow?"

He arched a single eyebrow. "I might be. Why do you ask?"

A coy smile, a hand running through her braided hair. "I thought I might come a-callin', to visit you again. That bourbon sure would taste fine."

"Well, well, you *is* looking for company, ain't you?"

"You strike me as a fine man." Her eyes narrowed. "Very fine."

"I am, I'll grant you that. You'll be grinning from cheek to cheek after I've finished with you." He stood up, a hand falling to his crotch. "If you get my meaning."

Licking her lips, White Dove's eyes did not move from the developing bulge in the soldier's trousers. She smiled. "What time shall I call?"

He filled his glass. "Round about now would be fine, sweet child. We'll have some fun together. I guarantee it."

"I shall look forward to it."

And she left, leaving the soldier chuckling to himself with self-satisfaction.

Chapter Eighteen

Tabatha slipped out of bed and crossed the room to the roughly-hewn cabinet beside the window. She threw water from the basin over her face and dried herself with a nearby towel. Naked, the goosebumps sprouted across her breasts but she did not care. The warmth of him lingered across her midriff and she closed her eyes at the memory. A man such as he could give her everything she ever wanted, ever needed. Perhaps, in return, he might fulfil her most pressing desire. To kill Simms.

She saw him in her mind's eye, the detective's lean body, his hands lifting her, easing himself inside her. Dodd was good, but Simms ... In another life, another world, they could have found love. But he used her, his passion, his thoughtfulness, all a sham. Out on the plains, with her father and stepmother leading them towards a so-called promised land, desperation forced them to do the unthinkable. They butchered their companions, a young family who joined them on the trail not two days out of the newly chartered city of Topeka. Vibrant, full of excitement for their journey east, they enthusiastically hitched up alongside Tabatha and her group and paid for so doing with their lives.

And Simms wanted to prosecute them for it.

Damn his hide! If only Annabelle's bullet had blown out his brains, life would be almost bearable. But Simms had shot her and Tabatha fled, bringing her here, to this stinking town, and this man. Dodd. A gunfighter. A man she would conquer, bind to her will. Smiling, she went back to the bed and snuggled up beside him, entwining her legs with his, kissing him on the neck. He moaned and turned to her and she smiled as his ardour grew, pressing itself against her belly. Yes, she would conquer him with ease.

* * *

Their room was on the first floor of the saloon, a dusty, cramped place, but the only choice available. Dodd stood at the window, tucking in his shirt and pulling on his coat. "After breakfast, I mean to find my old friend Dan."

"I don't know him," she said, stretching out her body under the single sheet.

Without turning, he adjusted his tie. "He's an old prospector. We met up in Fort Atkinson just before the army shipped out. Our plan was to head out west, head for Colorado, pitch a grub stake and dig for gold. I became somewhat embroiled in other business ... " He chuckled, turned and fitted his gun belt around his waist.

"Other business?"

"This and that."

"You don't give much away do you? I don't even know your first name."

He titled his head. "Yeah, but I know yours and that's all that matters." He eased his gun two or three times in its holster. "I think I'll call in on the sheriff first of all, see if he knows anything. Dan and I had an understanding. He sent me letters and the like, informing me of his whereabouts, but they dried out some months back. As my business affairs have been concluded, I decided to head out here, find out what was occurring, if anything. Went to place called Serenity, from where he sent me his last letter over six months ago, and they told me he'd packed up and headed out this way. So here I am. And here you are."

"Yes. Here I am. Why don't you take off those fancy clothes and show me how grateful you can be?"

He sniggered. "Lord love you, you are a hungry one, ain't you?"

"Sure am, especially when what's on the menu is the finest available."

He crossed to her, bending over to cup her breast whilst he kissed her. She moaned, groping for his crotch.

"God, Dodd, do it to me again, I'm begging you."

"When I get back," he said, breathless, stepping away. His eyes grew wide as she threw back the sheet to expose her body. "Dear God, woman, if you don't beat all."

Her hand snaked out. "Your business can wait." She licked her lips and bent one knee.

"Damn you," he gasped and ripped away at his belt, desperate.

She giggled with the ease of her victory.

Downstairs, Dodd found the bar empty so he slipped behind the counter and helped himself to a measure of brandy. Savouring the mellow taste, he rolled the smooth alcohol around inside his mouth before swallowing it down. He smacked his lips and held the glass up against the light from the main window and grunted with approval. As he drew the glass to his lips once more, something caught his attention from beyond the glass and, curious, he narrowed his eyes to try and make out the shapes moving about outside.

The man in soiled clothes, whom he'd met the previous day reading the news poster, was in agitated conversation with another. Dodd put down the unfinished brandy and pushed his way through the swing doors.

Pretending to take in the air, he pricked up one ear to catch the conversation, but succeeded in hearing the last sentence, screeched from the man in the soil-encrusted clothes: "Damn your eyes if it don't beat all – you talking this way to me riles me something awful!" Then he was gone, muttering a series of oaths and curses, striding across the street towards his horse.

"'Morning," said Dodd, touching the brim of his hat as the other man caught his eye.

"Do I know you?"

"Not sure," answered Dodd, keeping his eyes on the other as he mounted his ragged horse and set off. "Do you?"

Breathing hard, the man stepped up onto the boardwalk. He was a big man, shoulders somewhat stooped, arms thick, belly sagging over his gun belt. On his vest he wore a tin star. "I think I might check."

"You do that, sheriff." Dodd grinned, nodding towards the retreating back of the other man. "He seemed a mite agitated."

"What's that to you?"

"Nothing, 'cepting he might be of some interest to me."

"Is that so?"

"Yes, it is."

"Like to expand on that, mister?"

"Not really."

The sheriff pulled in a deep breath, stuck his thumbs in his waistband and regarded Dodd with a scowl. "What's your name?"

Dodd told him and the sheriff grunted. "I'm here looking for an old friend. Dan Stoakes."

"Dan? How do you know him?"

"Like I said – he's an old friend."

"You don't look like the sort of company a man like Dan would keep."

"Oh? And what sort of company might I be?"

"You look like a gunslinger to me, mister, the way you wear that there gun, your fancy rig. Might be you're a gambler or some such. I hear your type are moving out west, finding fortune in a hand of cards."

"Well, sorry to disappoint, but I ain't no gambler, at least not the kind you mean. But," he leaned forward, his smile oily slick, "I *am* a gunslinger. Run through your wanted posters, sheriff; you won't find me there, but send a wire across to Fort Atkinson and they'll let you know who I am. In the meantime, why don't you tell me where my dear friend Dan is at?"

Dodd saw the hesitation in the man's eyes, the slight trembling of the lips. They were signs he knew well.

"How do I know you're his friend?"

"Because I just told you."

"Mister, I don't truly know what your business is here, but I'm guessing it ain't good. We've already had a barrel load of trouble here in town. We don't need any more."

"You won't get none from me."

"I'm not so sure about that."

"You can trust me."

"Mister, my job is to protect this town. I see in you someone who is a close friend of trouble."

"My only friend, right now, is Dan."

"That's as maybe, but I'll ask you to—"

"Where is he?"

A tension gripped the air between the two men. The sheriff's previous bluster drained away as a change occurred, an uncertainty, something dangerous. The sheriff swallowed hard. "I don't know."

"Try a guess."

"He was in town a few days ago, making a claim, so I understand."

"A claim?"

"Assayer will give you the details, but mister, I do not think you should—"

"Sheriff, if I might give you some advice – you go about your business and I'll go about mine. We won't interfere with one another, I can promise you that. Unless," he winked and the sheriff gawped, "unless you is wanting to, of course. In which case, I'll oblige you."

Dodd's hand hovered close to his gun, but made no move towards it. The sheriff's eyes locked on the revolver and his voice quivered when he spoke. "No, I, er, don't think there will be a need for that."

"So we understand one another."

"Yes, we do."

"Then I'll wish you a good morning, sheriff."

For a moment, the sheriff hesitated but then, taking his cue from Dodd's cold, unblinking stare, he turned away and made his way down the boardwalk.

"What in the hell was all that?"

Dodd turned to see Tabatha leaning on the swing doors, her elbows across the top. "Just ironing out a few creases."

"That man is mean, but I ain't ever seen him back down like that before. You must have put the jitters into him; I'm not so sure if that was a wise thing to do."

Dodd shrugged. "It might stir up a few things. He told me Dan is here, which has to be a good thing. I'll visit the assayer's office and find out where Dan has his claim."

"You want some company?"

Smiling, he stepped over to her and kissed her softly on the mouth. "You need to get to work, young lady. I'll come a-calling when I'm all done."

"Don't be long, I'm missing you already."

He kissed her again. "You can cook me a fine dinner and, for dessert, I'll make you purr like a kitten."

Another kiss and she disappeared inside. Dodd paused for a moment, licked his lips and readjusted his pants, which had grown uncomfortably tight all of a sudden.

Chapter Nineteen

The main square, by mid-afternoon, buzzed with people going about their daily business. Despite the cold, dust billowed up from the wheels of passing wagons and horses and countless voices exchanged greetings as townsfolk criss-crossed from shop to eating house, from outfitters to merchant-stores. Drovers, pedlars, pilgrims came and went, using the Fort as a staging post for journeys further west or to sell their wares. Winter would soon pass, the promise of spring in the clear blue sky and the many flowers bursting forth amongst the surrounding hills. Glancing towards them and wishing she was there, White Dove, clutching the brown paper bag in both hands, gnawed away at her bottom lip, hoping no one would notice one small, insignificant Indian in this press of humanity.

Keeping her eyes set straight ahead, she strode across the square, struggling to maintain a nonchalant air. On reaching the door to the jailhouse, she took the chance to scan her surroundings. Nobody appeared to have noticed her, all of them too busy with their own business. The cold helped, with many wrapped up in their thick coats, too intent on keeping warm than wasting time on a solitary squaw. Giving a wry smile, she turned and opened the door.

She froze.

The guard behind the desk, long legs crossed over the top, was not the same one as before. Her stomach lurched and for a moment she was undecided what to do – to enter, or make a hasty retreat.

"And what can I do you for?" He swung his legs away and stood up. He was tall, a young soldier, clean shaven, smooth-faced, nothing like the other.

White Dove tried her best not to swallow too hard and raised the bag. "I was hoping to meet with the other guard, the one normally on duty."

"Larry? Hell, Larry is late – Larry is *always* late. You had a date with him?" He came around the desk, hands on hips, studying her. "I can see why."

Despite her best efforts, she felt the heat rise to her cheeks and she looked away, as coyly as she could manage.

"And what's that? A present?"

He reached out and took the bag, pulling it apart to peer inside. He pursed his lips in obvious pleasure.

"I brought it for him. Larry, I mean. To have a drink. A good time."

"Did you now?" The soldier lifted out the bottle and held it up, reading the label. "Well, this is his tipple all right. But, like I say, he's late." He placed the bottle on the desk. "I'm not so sure the Major would take too kindly to Larry drinking on duty, truth be told."

"I won't say anything, not if you won't."

"Little lady, what Larry does in his spare time is up to him, but this ain't no spare time." He jabbed his finger towards the cell. "That bastard in there killed one of our boys, for which he is gonna hang. Beat the living hell out of another one of us. Can't say I know much else because I wasn't there, but this much I will say – it is our sworn duty to guard him, keep him cooped up until the day of reckoning comes. Larry has his orders, and drinkin' don't feature in them, so best if I—"

"Killed two of your boys?" She gaped and turned her head to the crumpled body in the far corner of the cell.

"Just the one. Shot a trooper in the back of the head, cowardly bastard that he is. My friends say it was all over a woman." His eyes narrowed. "A squaw."

She held up both her hands. "It was not me. I am a friend of Larry, not that … that *killer* in there."

"Well, that's as maybe, but from where I'm standing I'd say—"

The jailhouse door flew open and in strode Larry, his heavy frame enveloped in a voluminous army greatcoat, pounding himself with his gloved hands. A great stream of smoky breath poured out of his mouth and he saw White Dove, "Hot dang, if you didn't come!"

"So, you know this … woman?"

Larry frowned towards the other soldier. ""Course I do, you dimwit. We is friends, ain't we darlin'?"

She smiled her answer in the affirmative.

"And that, I do believe, is mine." Larry pushed past his fellow soldier and scooped up the bottle. "You weren't fixing on muscling in on me, were you, Daniel?"

"No, I was not," snapped Daniel, some of the colour leaving his face. "She ain't my type."

"Well, ain't that just *convenient.*"

"What in the hell does that mean?"

"Anything you want it to, but I wouldn't put anything past you. You've run me a merry dance with women on more than one occasion."

"That's your memory all fuddled with whisky, Larry. Don't you go accusing me of something I ain't done."

"Might be you was *meaning* to do something, eh? After all, she is a pretty little one, don't you think?"

"Larry, you do as you please. As far as I am concerned, none of this is my concern." He went over to the far wall and pulled down his coat from one of the hooks there. "Like I said to your little friend here, we is duty bound to guard this prisoner. I know I have fulfilled my part."

"You are one self-righteous old woman, Daniel, do you know that? Duty? Jesus, here we are, stuck in the middle of nowhere, with the cold freezing our asses off, pay not forthcoming, news of trouble with Indians and the like, and you expect me to worry about duty?" He sneered, tore out the stopper from the bottle and took a long drink.

Shaking his head, Daniel fastened up his coat and crammed his hat down over his forehead. "I'll leave you to it," he said and went out, slamming the door behind him.

"He seems mad."

"He's an asshole, that's what he is." He cocked his head and grinned. "I thought you might have forgotten about what we said."

"How could I?" she said, moving closer.

He gripped her around the waist. Planting a palm on his chest, she leaned back and tapped the bottle he still held with her free hand. "I brought you that as a little present."

His face split into a wide grin. "That's sweet of you. You really are a gift from heaven."

With his attention given over to the contents of the bottle, she moved over to the cell and peered into the tiny interior. Simms lay slumped on his narrow cot, still huddled up, his breathing sounding strained. "He has not long recovered from his illness," she said without turning. "He needs more blankets."

"Ah, to hell with him. He hasn't moved since you were last here. My guess is his ribs are busted." She turned to watch him tipping the bottle to his lips. He took a huge swallow, gasping as he brought it down again. "Dang, that is good."

"Only the best," she said, giving a slight, alluring smile, "*for* the best."

He put the bottle down on the desk and went to her, cupping one of her breasts in his hand whilst he stroked her hair with the other. "My, you are a pretty one. Is he your man?"

She glanced towards Simms, then looked at Larry again. "He was. Now, I think I have another. A better one."

"You're damn right." He leaned into her and they kissed. Pulling back, he licked his lips, eyes misting over. "We have to be careful, mind. I don't want Daniel barging back in." He went over to the door and took a quick look outside before stepping back inside to lock it. The sound of tumblers engaging rang loud in that small jailhouse room. "We don't want to be disturbed."

Larry turned and went white, mouth dropping open. He tried to yelp, but too late. White Dove hit him full across the face with the whisky bottle, the glass smashing, drenching him in alcohol and lacerating his flesh. He screamed, hands instinctively clutching at the erupting wounds and crumpled to his knees. Without a moment's pause, she reached for his gun and pulled it from the holster.

"Don't kill him."

She whirled around to see Simms gripping the bars, his face blackened from the many blows he'd received.

"I want to."

"I know. But don't. The gunshot will alert the whole damn fort. Hit him across the head, get the keys and set me free."

She followed his orders without question, cracking the revolver hard across the squirming guard's head. One blow wasn't enough; she hit him twice more before he grew quiet, a tiny murmur accompanying the bubbling blood oozing from the cuts around his face, a new trail springing from his broken nose.

Crossing to the desk, she swept up the keys. There were three of them and, within seconds, Simms was free, embracing her. She held onto him, as tight as she dared given the state he was in, and bit down her tears.

He took the gun and checked it. "They locked mine away somewhere, so this will have to do." He shot a glance towards Larry. "This is as bad a mess as I've been in."

"They said you killed one of them – shot him in the head."

"You know that isn't true."

"Yes, but who would say you did such a thing?"

"I don't know, but clearly someone doesn't want me in the way."

She frowned. "In the way of what?"

"I don't know that either." He lifted up the set of keys. "I'll slip out the back, get my horse and make my way back to Glory. You go back to the room, finish packing our things, then leave. You follow the trail, and don't deviate from it. There's a small, narrow gorge a day's ride from here, with high bluffs on either side. I'll meet you there. Don't speak to anyone." She smiled and fell into his arms and he squeezed her tight. "When we get there, I'll send a telegram to Johnstone, explaining everything."

"You think he will believe you?"

"He has to – otherwise I'm the one thing I never wanted to be. A killer on the run."

Chapter Twenty

Exchanged glances, some hostile, most curious, greeted Melody as she went down to the stream to clean the clothes Long Elk threw at her as a way of greeting her good morning. She lay under her buffalo skin, watching him as he dressed, the muscles in his torso and thighs rippling. She did not believe a man could look so fine. Such a thought, however, did nothing to dampen down her hatred for him and, throughout the night, she had sat pressed up against the side of the tepee, gripping a knife, daring him to try and move another inch closer. He did not, throwing himself under his own cover instead, grunting his frustration, and soon fell asleep. With his snores echoing around the confines of their canvas home, Melody eventually allowed herself to drift away.

She awoke with a start when he hurled clothes across her face. He said something, pulled on his leggings and went out into the daylight.

And now here she was, with the other squaws, the old, the young, the thin and frail, the hearty and strong, but all of them native Indians. She knew, by the way they stared, she would never be one of them.

She soon learned what to do, studying the way they pounded their own washing piles with stones, slapping them over boulders, rubbing them under the running water. Her own efforts took longer, but when she held up her efforts, she took a certain degree of pride in seeing all the stains gone.

A woman spoke to her, her strange language ringing out, sing-song fashion. She strained to understand, to catch something familiar, but, failing, she merely shrugged, offering an apologetic smile. Others stepped forward, cackling, and from their gestures and their tone, she realised this was animosity at its worst.

Returning to the camp, she caught sight of Long Elk, standing together with half a dozen other braves and another man, different to the rest, albeit he too appeared to be an Indian. He wore store bought trousers, a checked shirt and a floppy brimmed hat that should have belonged on the head of a soldier. She studied him for a little too long, for when Long Elk noticed her, he rushed over and struck her back-handed across the jaw. She dropped to the ground, the clothes spilling amongst the dirt. Long Elk kicked them away, undoing all of her labours. He barked in her direction and she flinched, shying away as if each syllable were another blow. When at last he went back to his friends, she gathered up the clothes and saw the stranger looking in her direction. The ghost of a smile flickered across his mouth, but then he too returned to their animated conversation.

In the chill of the evening, the men sat around the huge campfire, laughing, exchanging stories, drinking from animal skin gourds. She watched them from the entrance of the tepee and considered running off into the night. If they were drunk, they may not notice her absence until she was far away. But then a coyote howled in the distance and she knew it was hopeless – even if she did make it out of the camp, the thought of becoming food for wild animals terrified her. So, shoulders slumping in despair, she went back inside and huddled up beneath the buffalo skin.

When he came in, some hours later, and mauled at her, his whiskey-sodden breath drenching her, turning her stomach, she put her knee in his groin and pushed him away. He screamed at her and, despite the darkness, she saw his eyes flash white before he fell through the flap and emptied the contents of his guts into the ground beyond. She waited, wishing to God she had the knife. But it was gone, lost together with her hopes, her life. She sat up, pulling her knees to her chest and rocked herself, weeping openly. When he returned he stood, breathing hard.

"You are my woman," he said, voice low, and for a moment she stopped, shocked he knew English. As the seconds slipped by, she readied herself for an assault. It never came and he fell down, belched, pulled his cover over his head and slept.

The feeble moonlight seeped through the crack of the flap, casting its silver light over the form of his body and she looked and wished she was dead.

At the river, she repeated her chores from the day before, washing away Long Elk's vomit from the previous night. No one looked her way this time. Perhaps they knew of what passed between her and Long Elk – or, more correctly, what had not passed. Whatever the truth, she concentrated on scrubbing clean his vest, rubbing the material through her hands until the fibres almost parted. Only then did she stop and sit back. It was then she saw him.

The stranger who visited the camp.

He sat astride a pinto pony on the far side of the stream, hatless, hair hanging loose, a carbine in one hand. His eyes held hers and again he smiled, more openly this time. Something crossed between them. She stood up, mesmerised, and he steered his pony through the shallow water, making no attempt to disguise his approach. The other women stood, some raising their voices in greeting, but soon these turned to cries of alarm. Something was wrong here. They broke as one, leaving their washing behind, sprinting up the bank, kicking up dust and mud.

Voices came to her from the camp but Melody cared nothing for them. The stranger reined his pony and held out his hand, beckoning her to approach. As if in a dream, she stepped forward, but stopped when the cold water hit her feet. Jerking her head around, she saw them, three warriors, bounding forward and, at their lead, Long Elk.

"Take my hand."

She snapped around to this mysterious man and then, without another pause, she gripped his arm and hauled herself up behind him. As he turned his mount, Long Elk leaped forward. He was screaming; anger, disbelief, desperation, she didn't know which, nor did she care. The stranger turned the carbine and it belched fire, the bullet hitting the warrior in the throat, throwing him backwards as if he were a piece of limp cloth. He hit the bank with a grunt then rolled down into the water, clawing at the gaping wound, a horrible gurgling erupting from his mouth. There was no time to look or consider what might happen next and, before she realised, the stranger was beating at his pony's rump with the carbine, driving it through the water with all its strength whilst behind. The other warriors waded towards them, knives and hatchets aloft.

She held onto the man's sides, buried her head into his back and prayed they would survive.

And when she opened her eyes it was to find her prayers answered; the pony, having reached the far bank, plunged into the cover of the trees and negotiated its way to freedom.

Chapter Twenty-One

"What in the hell is that, Silas?"

The sheriff, squatting down on his haunches, lifted up the garment in both hands and pursed his lips. "A coat."

The deputy rubbed his chin. "Are you thinking maybe the killer snagged it on this broken fence as he made his getaway?"

"That's exactly right, Vaughn."

"But hell, there must a hundred men who own a coat like that."

"Yeah." Silas licked his lips and stood up, the coat draped over one arm and, in his hand, a screwed up, dog-eared piece of paper. "But not all of them leave a letter in their pocket."

Vaughn gawped. "Is his name on it?"

Silas threw Vaughn the coat and unfolded the paper. "It's a claim form. From the assayer. And here are their names, written as bold as you like." He brought it up and showed it to his deputy, who shook his head, stunned. "I'll go visit the assayer's office and find out where this claim is. With any luck they'll still be there. In the meantime, you round up a posse of half a dozen and swear 'em in. I'll meet you at my office within the hour."

"I'll need more than an hour to muster six men, Silas."

"Just do it, Vaughn. I'm quit pussyfooting around, you get me? These sons-of-bastards are gonna pay, one way or the other."

"You mean—"

"I *mean*, you gather up them boys – I think you'll have more than six, all of 'em eager to shoot these bastards dead."

"They might even lynch 'em."

Silas grinned and put the paper into his jacket pocket. "Yeah. And who would give a damn, eh?"

Dodd rode out of town without a word to Tabatha. The clerk at the office was more than forthcoming about where Dan's stake was, despite his initial reluctance to divulge its exact whereabouts. Dodd chuckled. You can almost count on a Remington revolver, primed, ready to fire and pointed directly at a man's head to get the information required.

Some distance from town, he took his horse up a narrow pass into the mountains, taking his time, careful not to lead his animal into danger. The pass, narrow and twisting, was well worn and, in parts, fell away. At these points he dismounted, leading the animal by the reins, testing each step before putting his weight fully down on the broken ground. When the path finally descended towards the river, Dodd breathed a prolonged sigh of relief but continued to tread carefully.

Trees clung to the river bank and, in parts, they grew thick, the sunlight unable to penetrate the gloom caused by the close proximity of gnarled trunks. In places the branches interlaced so heavily it was difficult to distinguish one tree from its neighbour, the almost perfect location from which to spring an ambush. Every few paces, Dodd paused and peered into the darkness, senses straining, sometimes half-imagining Indians lurked within, watching, waiting. Forcing himself on, to bring himself some reassurance, he eased his revolver in and out of its holster.

And then he spotted the camp.

He tied his horse to a nearby tree and eased out the carbine from its scabbard beside the saddle. Checking it, he patted the horse's muzzle and moved forward, keeping low, eyes scanning the surroundings.

There was a tent of sorts, erected next to a ramshackle collection of mining tools, a still smoking campfire with a black pot suspended over the feeble heat. A mule grazed on the far side and made no movement as Dodd crept forward. The sound of the passing river disguised any noise he may have made and, when the animal caught sight of him, its single response was a slight flicking of one ear. Dodd, holding his breath, inched forward with extreme caution. He noted the stakes hammered into the ground and followed their course, stopping only to peek inside the tent. Finding it empty, a few old blankets and pieces of clothing the only items within, he moved on.

Soon he caught sight of the tiny mound identifying the area of Ben's strike. Here, the trees were few, nothing more than a scattering of dried up twigs and, cut into the rocky side of the riverbank, a large hole, disappearing into blackness. He remained motionless, eyes locked on the opening, sucking in his lips, undecided what to do next. One thing gnawed away at him and caused him to waver – where were their horses?

Rummaging through a collection of papers, the clerk, spectacles perched on the end of his nose, returned to the counter, shaking his head. "Funny thing is, since the murder, a lot of people seem interested in this claim, sheriff. I'm not fully convinced that the find is all that big, but nevertheless—"

"Others have shown interest? You mean the ones on this here copy?" he waved the paper he found in the discarded coat under the clerk's nose.

"Not just them. I didn't deal with their initial claim, as you know; I'm still taking my time in sorting out everything, but I will say that—"

"I just need to know who else is interested, goddamnit."

The clerk paled and took a small step backwards. "Sheriff, there ain't no point becoming vexed. I'm trying to do the best I can here, but I was called in at short notice by the company

… " He looked away from the Sheriff's blazing gaze. "There was a smart looking fella in here, not an hour or so ago, wanting to know the whereabouts of Stoakes' claim."

"And you told him?"

"He wasn't exactly the sort of person you say 'no' to, if I'm being honest."

"A lean looking fella, well dressed in frock coat, silver lined waistcoat, a pistol strapped to his thigh? A livid scar running all the way down one side of his face?"

The man swallowed hard. "With the most penetrating, unsettling eyes I've ever seen – yes, he was the fella."

Silas pushed his hat back on his head and shot a glance towards the deputy accompanying him. "Jeez, and you told him?"

"Like I said, I wasn't about to hold out on such a fella, Sheriff. Besides, he said he was an old friend of Dan's."

"All right. And Dan's stake, it was the same as this one?" Again he brandished the paper.

"Close enough to it, yes. But, like I say, that area has been well surveyed in the past – there's little chance of there being anything of any real worth out there. Unless something was missed."

"Looks like that is the case, don't it just."

Silas sighed and turned on his heels, stomping out of the office with barely contained rage.

"Damn it all to hell," he said, staring towards the sky, running his tongue along his lips, deep in thought.

"What's eating you, Sheriff?"

Silas blinked and glared towards his other deputy. "What's *eating* me? What's eating me, Vince, is that we are going up against two hard-boiled murderers *and* the most dangerous man I think has ever lived – that's what's *fucking eating me*, Vince."

He sat on the riverbank, watching the gurgling water flow gently by. The rustle of the wind through the tree branches on the far side caught his attention and for a moment he allowed his mind to drift back to happier times. A warmth came over him, despite the cold, biting air, and he smiled. Tabatha brought back some of those feelings, the promise of a life, free from pain, free from struggle. A woman like that could warm him at night, bring him sunshine in the day. A little place somewhere, a bunch of pigs, a garden full of potatoes and the like. Nothing fancy, a place to settle, grow.

Something came through the undergrowth, fallen branches snapping, the sound reverberating throughout the glade and heralding the approach of someone. Dodd gathered up his carbine in a rush, rolling over towards a small rocky outcrop and pressed himself against the far side, shielding himself from the tree line from where the noise came.

He waited, controlling his breathing, straining to hear. Another snap, more movement. He forced himself to remain out of sight, even when the snort of a horse exploded from the far side. They might be Indians, mounted on ponies, or the men returning to their camp. Either way, there was a fight coming, so Dodd readied himself, his heart pounding but his fingers perfectly under control when he eased back the hammer of his carbine and prepared himself for the killing to begin.

Chapter Twenty-Two

Stepping out from the telegram office, Dixon again read the brief message and cursed silently to himself. The first one, which arrived a few days before, he hoped would be forgotten. All he need do was ignore it. Unfortunately, this course proved unsound and here he was, with another summons spat out from Twin Buttes, asking him to help them in the apprehension of two vicious killers. Folding up the message, he slipped it inside his tail coat and descended the steps. He paused to roll himself a cigarette and glanced around as another hectic day played itself out before him.

They were changing the guard at the main gate, the soldiers exchanging a few jokes, laughing out loud. A man in buckskin passed through, leading a team of two pack mules, laden down with pelts. Three Indians were in close conversation with two other men, gesticulating wildly, none of them looking pleased. Wagons rolled in and rolled out, men on horseback, women guiding teams of horses, pilgrims moving further west. A scene which had remained unchanged for well over two or more decades, and one Dixon always hoped to profit from. Circumstances changed his entire perspective, but the arrival of Simms might just give him another avenue to explore.

He cast his mind back to an hour or so earlier when he'd gone to the jail to try to speak to the detective, wanting to know if he had any information regarding the incident at the staging station. Perhaps the news of the fire had pricked his curiosity. Dixon didn't know, but he was not prepared to take any chances. If Simms had sent a telegram to his main office in Illinois, God alone knew what the fallout might be. But when he went up to the jail door, what he saw sent a chill through him and any notion of talking with the Pinkerton evaporated. Simms was gone, the cell now holding a blood-spattered soldier, lying in the corner, groaning like a wounded animal.

Dixon worked fast, doing his best not to look too conspicuous as he walked along towards Clancy's. At this time of the morning, the fort had yet to fully raise itself for the day ahead. Few people were inside and none of them paid him attention. A handful of bleary eyed prospectors, salesmen, drifters and pilgrims milling around their dining tables taking coffee. And O'Shaughnessy, legs stretched out, head lolling on his chest.

"He's gone," said Dixon without preamble, slumping down in the chair opposite his associate.

O'Shaughnessy mumbled something, sat up and wiped his mouth with the back of his hand. "Jesus, what time would it be?"

"Did you hear what I said?"

"No. Did you hear me? I need a drink." He raised his hand, clicking his fingers several times to catch the attention of the barkeep. "I was with a couple of lively lads last night, and we sort of—"

"Listen to me, for God's sake – Simms has gone."

O'Shaughnessy frowned, "*Gone*? What does that mean, gone where?"

"Broke out, escaped, skedaddled, call it what you will, but he has gone, leaving some poor bastard in his place behind the bars of his cell."

"Well how in the fuck did he manage that?"

"How do I know, but he's done it. Listen," he leaned forward and stopped as the barkeep loomed over, placing a full glass of whisky on the table. Dixon waited until the man was out of earshot before he continued. "We have to track him down. If he gets back to his town and starts up an investigation, we're fucked. You understand me?"

"He can't prove a thing. Besides, if he broke out, he's a fugitive. They'll track him down, bring him back and hang him. Escaping is an admission of guilt." He picked up the glass, closed his eyes in expectation and downed it in one. He beamed, "Best bloody breakfast there is. You should try it. Might help you see things more clearly."

"We can't take the risk. He's trained, has all sorts of skills we know nothing about, so we can't underestimate him, not for a moment." He looked around, checking nobody could hear. "I want you to get after him. You and your men. He can't have gotten far. When you find him, you kill him. Understand? We can't take the risk of him getting away. If we're to undercut Danks and make good our investment in the stage company, Simms has to die."

O'Shaughnessy sat there, silent, studying Dixon for a long time. "You really think he has the wherewithal to find out what we've been doing?"

"Absolutely."

"How do you know? Maybe he's like all of the rest – a hick who couldn't give a tuppenny damn."

"No, he's different. I asked around. This guy is a bulldog, I tell you – he never lets go. He's come up against a series of mean villains and has bettered every one of them. If he gets back to his town, he'll be in touch with his bosses back in Chicago and they'll send an army out here to investigate why that staging post burnt down. And that, my friend, we cannot allow to happen."

"All right," breathed O'Shaughnessy, curling up his lips, "I'll get ready. Just tell me – you want him dead, out there in the prairie? No witnesses, nothing at all."

"I want you to kill him and bury him, or burn him, or whatever you need to do. I want it to be as if he never even existed."

O'Shaughnessy grinned and adjusted his belt. "Just how I like it."

Now, with O'Shaughnessy and three other dangerous looking men having left the fort, Dixon tried his best to relax. When he went to the telegraph office to check if Simms had indeed sent a cable, he almost hugged the clerk with relief when he discovered the detective had not. But, when the man thrust another message into his hand, and Dixon read it, the black cloud came down again.

Something caught his eyes and broke into his thoughts. From out of the barracks a man strode, a junior officer by the look of him. Clean shaven, youthful, keen. Beside him, another soldier, springing up and down as if every step pressed his feet down on red-hot coals. They made their way quickly towards the jailhouse and Dixon frowned. The jailhouse held Simms, beaten half to death – or so they believed – due to the recent shooting. Taking a few moments, he lit his cigarette and wandered across the square to the jailhouse.

He'd been there before, of course, not an hour since, but now, at the open door, he peered inside to see the two soldiers standing in abject horror at what they witnessed. Dixon made a good show of being surprised. "Holy shit in a bucket, this cannot be happening!"

The young officer was white, hands thrust against his hips, staring through the bars into the cell and turned his neck to stare, aghast, at Dixon. "He's gone."

"I can't find the keys." The private was searching through the desk with increasing desperation, throwing away papers strewn over the tabletop in all directions. He ripped open drawers and rifled through and his face, when it came up, was red with anger. His gaze settled on Dixon standing in the doorway. "What the fuck do you want?"

"Thought I might be of service," Dixon said, stepping inside. His boots crushed the glass sprayed out across the floor and he looked down, noting the spots of blood. "Seems like a breakout to me."

"You don't say?"

Dixon smiled towards the private, his face flushed with rage. Before another word, the lieutenant stepped up. "You know about any of this?"

"I think I might."

"Well, I think you should tell me what it is you know, Marshal."

"Yes, I shall. I'll tell it all to Major Porter."

The lieutenant grunted and turned on the private. "Get this place tidied up. The keys must be somewhere. Then get that miserable bag of shit out of there and find out what the hell went on." He looked again at Dixon. "Lead the way, Marshal."

Chapter Twenty-Three

The splashing grew louder, the sound of horses moving through the shallow waters, a man's voice urging the animals on. Dodd waited, biding his time, knowing once he made his play it needed to be quick and decisive.

More urging, horse flanks being slapped, hooves digging into the muddy bank.

"Come on, goddamnit." White men's voices. The knowledge brought Dodd a tiny relaxing of the shoulders, as his worst fear was to encounter Indians out here. He sucked in a breath, gritted his teeth and sprang to his feet.

He took a bead on the lead rider, shooting him in the chest with the carbine, blowing him rearwards over the saddle and pitching him in the water.

All hell broke loose.

Both horses reared up, panicking, eyes wild, screaming, desperate to flee. The riderless horse proved the most spooked, crashing through the water to the bank and galloping off into the distance. Meanwhile, the second rider fought for control, but the fight was uneven, his animal terrified. He tried to pull out his holstered gun but already Dodd was moving forward, his own revolver in his hand; he shot the man in the thigh. The rider screamed louder even than the horses and toppled sideways into the churned-up river.

Dodd waded across, pausing only to check the first rider was dead. He then grabbed the wounded one by the collar and hauled him towards the bank. The man fought, lashing out with his fist, twisting in Dodd's grip, but the pain from the bullet in his leg overcame him and he lapsed into unconsciousness, the shock too much for his body to resist.

As a dead weight, Dodd's struggle to haul the man out of the river almost defeated him. Gritting his teeth, he managed to place both hands under the man's armpits and strain to bring him up onto dry land. He collapsed next to his burden, mouth gaping open, taking in huge gulps of air. Drenched in water and sweat, chest heaving, he waited until his recovery was almost complete, then he sat up and stared down at the unconscious man. The blood seeped out of his wounded thigh and Dodd knew his chances of survival were slim; he'd need to work fast.

Down at the water's edge, Dodd filled his hat with water and returned to pour it over the man's face. Coughing and spluttering, hands thrashing, flailing away imaginary blows, he moaned loudly, "Damned bastard."

Without speaking, Dodd leaned over and relieved him of the gun at his hip. He tossed it into the river.

"Oh dear God Almighty, I'm shot," the man said, clutching at his leg. With each passing second, his face grew paler.

"Tie your bandana around it and pull tight."

The man gaped at Dodd and spat, "Fuck you, you murdering bastard. Who in the hell are you and what have shot me up for?"

Dodd rocked back on his haunches, considering the man for a moment before drawing his revolver and pointing it towards him. "Tie up your leg, or you'll be dead within thirty minutes."

No doubt convinced by this, the man deftly did as Dodd advised, ripping away the sodden bandana around his neck and fastening it above the wound. He snarled, jerking his head back in pain as he drew the two ends of the neckerchief tightly together. Once recovered, sucking in ragged breaths, he tied it off and Dodd grunted with satisfaction as the trail of running blood slowed.

"I'm gonna die, ain't I?"

"Not if I get you to a doctor, get that piece of lead out and stitch up the hole."

"A doctor? What in the hell? Who *are you*?"

Dodd shrugged. "You tell me what I need to know, and I'll take you back into town, get you fixed up real good." He nodded towards the running water. "Can't help your friend. He's dead."

"Charlie was a good man, and you killed him."

"Yes I did. I'll do the same for you if you don't tell me what I need to know."

The man squirmed, tears springing from the corners of his eyes as he pressed his hands over the wound. "Jesus, this hurts. I don't think I can walk."

"Don't you fret about that – I'll help you, put you on the back of your mule in your camp. We'll be in town under three hours and by this evening you'll be tucked up in bed, all safe and warm."

The man's eyes widened. "You're crazy, that's what you are. You murder Charlie, shoot me, then talk about getting me patched up?"

"*If* you tell me what I want to know." Dixon's voice remained flat and neutral throughout. It now developed a meaner, harder edge when he said, "Where's Dan?"

The man did a double-take, his frown growing deep. "Dan? Who the hell is he?"

"The man who staked this claim, the man who found the silver. Dan Stoakes."

"I don't know of any Dan Stoakes. Mister, you've made a mistake – a *big* mistake."

"You staked out this claim? Is that what you're telling me?"

"Fair and square."

"So how come the assayer's office has Dan's name all over the original claim?"

For a moment, it seemed to Dodd the wounded man would crumple up and burst into tears. His face sagged, expression convulsed in pain, eyes squeezed tight. "Oh shit, that was nothing. Nothing at all, really."

"Nothing at all, eh? Friend, you'd best tell me the truth or I swear to God I'll leave you."

The expression changed again, the pain slipping away, replaced by terror. "You wouldn't do that."

"I killed your friend, didn't I? I'm your worst nightmare, friend." He put the barrel of his revolver close to the wound. "Perhaps I should remind you of the sort of agony you're gonna be experiencing after I leave you."

He pushed the barrel into the wound, grunting with the effort; the man's body went into spasm, back going rigid, legs stretching out as if yanked by invisible ropes. And he screamed. High-pitched, a horrible sound, ringing through the surroundings and disappearing into the trees.

Dodd eased the pressure and the man collapsed back into the earth, gasping, head lolling from side to side, "Oh Jesus, please. *Please.*"

"I ain't gonna ask again."

His words came as garbled mess, filled with terror and pain, "I don't know him, I swear it. Mister, if I did, I would tell you. If you'd only just—"

Dodd repeated his cruel attack, prolonging it this time, leaning into the move, pressing the barrel deeper still. The man screamed, as before, his hands this time sinking into the muddy ground, body writhing, kicking out, trying to roll away from the pressure, the awful searing agony.

"All right, all right," he squawked and Dodd drew back the gun and the man collapsed again, rolling over onto his side, holding onto the pumping wound.

"Next time I won't stop."

The man turned and looked, feverish eyes bewildered, filled with despair. "Please, I'm begging you. I'll tell you, I promise."

"Pull that bandana tighter," said Dodd, sitting back. He took off his own neckerchief and wiped the barrel of his gun. He clicked his tongue a few times. "You sure do bleed a lot, boy. Now, where's Dan?"

"I'll tell you, tell you as it was. We met him in town, the morning he made his claim, and we got to talking. He told us he needed help, help with digging out the silver. So we rode here with him, Charlie and me. Oh sweet Jesus," he grimaced, gripping the leg hard. "It hurts, damn you to hell."

"Keep talking."

"You're an evil bastard, that's what you is."

Dodd motioned with his gun, and the man yelped. "All right, damn you. All right." He sucked in a deep breath, swallowing down a new wave of pain before continuing. "We set to working and everything was going just swell, then one morning he gets up and says he's going to town, and that is the last we saw of him, I swear to God."

"So where'd he go?"

"I have no idea, mister. No idea. He just got up and went." He bent forward from the waist, hissing through his teeth as more pain seized him. "I think I'm gonna die, damn you."

"Problem is, I don't believe you."

"Well, I don't really give a good damn what you believe. He's gone and that is the end of it. Now, you get me to that doctor like you said you would."

"What did you do with him, you snivelling piece of shit." This time, Dodd rammed the muzzle of the revolver straight into the man's forehead. "I'll shoot you dead right now. What did you do with him?"

Blubbering, the man's defences gave way, mouth turning slack, "Oh no, no please, you can't do that. I told you the truth, I truly did."

"Then you can tell it to Saint Peter, 'cause I'm gonna blow your brains out."

"All right," his arms came up, stretching skywards, "all right. It was Charlie. Charlie followed him that morning and I heard the gunshot and I knew it. Knew it, I tell you, knew what he'd done. Then he came back into camp and I saw it in his eyes. Like a wild man he was, cussing and snapping away like a turtle, all worked up with the killing and all."

"And was it the same back in town? With that family you murdered?"

"Oh Jesus, that wasn't me. I told Charlie, I told him, truly I did, not to go and do such a thing, but Charlie, he was not right-minded. He was a dumb-assed son-of-a—"

Dodd squeezed the trigger and shot him dead, putting the bullet into the man's brain, blowing the back of his head off.

For a long time afterwards Dodd sat, clearing his mind of what the morning had brought, but one thing he could not erase – the dreadful thought of not knowing where poor old Dan lay, cold and alone in the unforgiving ground.

Chapter Twenty-Four

In his quarters, Major Porter strode up and down, face flushed. "Damn it all, when the Colonel hears of this he'll put my balls in a noose."

"Don't quite understand your thought processes there, Major," said Dixon, leaning against the wall, arms folded. Next to him, the young lieutenant stood ramrod straight, glaring at him. "Listen, I never truly believed Simms was capable of doing such a thing – shooting a man in the back simply ain't his style."

Porter stopped pacing and took up rubbing his chin. "That's what I'm afraid the Colonel will think. Holy shit, I should have investigated further before I let those mad dogs beat the hell out of him."

"Well, that's all water under now, Major. Whoever or however Simms got out of that jail cell, O'Shaughnessy got wind of it and is after him, hoping to kill him somewhere out on the prairie. Problem is, I don't think that dumb Irishman knows what he's going up against."

"And you do, I suppose?"

"Major, we both know the reputation Simms carries around with him like a second skin. The man is a hard-boiled killer. O'Shaughnessy is a thug. I was biding my time, waiting for him to slip before I arrested him, but now this . . . " He shook his head.

"My guess is Simms will kill him, then make it back to his town of Bovey."

"But he still has a charge to answer."

"Maybe, maybe not. Colonel Johnstone won't buy it, and neither do I. I believe he was set-up by O'Shaughnessy."

"For what purpose?"

Dixon turned to look at the lieutenant. "That's why I'll ride over to Bovey and question Simms at length. He must have caught O'Shaughnessy doing something he shouldn't have. I'll find out, don't worry."

The lieutenant frowned. "You seem to know a good deal of what's been going on around here, Marshal."

"That's my job son, or have you forgotten where duty lies?"

The lieutenant tensed and took a step forward.

"Now hold on, Miers," snapped Porter. "The marshal here talks a good deal of sense. This is what I propose – you accompany the marshal here to Bovey and help question Simms, then you can—"

"*Me*?" blurted out the young officer, "With all due respect, Major, I don't think—"

"You'll do as you are ordered, Lieutenant Miers. Now get your things packed. I want you both out of here within the hour."

Dixon gave a little cough and produced the folded-up telegram given to him earlier. "I have some unfinished duties to attend to first, Major. I received this cable, apparently the second such request, the first having gone astray somehow. An unsolved murder in the town of Twin Buttes requires my attention."

"Damn your investigations, Dixon. You'll cut across country and try to head off Simms. I want this heap of shit parcelled up and put away before the Colonel returns. If that means you killing that interfering bastard, then so be it."

"I ain't no assassin, Major."

"No, and you ain't no angel of mercy either. Lieutenant, go and saddle your horse."

Lieutenant Miers went to speak but, thinking better of it, brought up his hand in a salute and went out. Porter crossed to the door and made sure it was closed. He then looked across to Dixon. "I won't mince words, Dixon. I'll make it worth your while if you make this go away."

"Meaning?"

"Meaning, I'll give you one hundred dollars to tidy this all up."

Dixon snorted, "Jesus, you must be awful scared of what the Colonel will say."

"The Colonel will move to have me decommissioned, Marshal, and I ain't in no hurry to see that happen. You bring back O'Shaughnessy, Simms, or both of them, but you bring them back and put an end to this business, you hear me."

"I hear you. But if you make it two hundred, I can guarantee an acceptable outcome for all involved."

"Meaning what?"

Dixon nodded towards the door. "Oh, I think you know. That boy is a mite keen. My guess is he'll tell Johnstone everything anyway."

"I'll pretend I didn't hear any of what you're suggesting, Marshal."

"Pretend what you will, you just give me the money. A hundred now, a further hundred on my return."

Porter rubbed his chin again, the conflict within etched into every worry line on his face. "Very well. Do what you think best. In the meantime—"

"In the meantime, you just give me the money."

Porter blew out a loud breath and crossed over to a cabinet pushed against the far wall. Apart from his desk, it was the only other piece of furniture in that sparse, grey walled room. Not even a picture broke up the drab surroundings.

As Porter pulled out a drawer, the door burst open and Miers exploded into the room, eyes wide, blowing hard.

Porter rounded on him, furious. "What in the name of—"

"Begging your pardon, Major, but we got him out."

"Got him out? Who did you get out of where?"

"Stoober, sir, in the jail cell."

"You got him … Well where in the hell does that give you cause to—"

"He's told us how Simms got out, sir." He looked from the Major to Dixon, and back again. "It was his squaw, sir. Hit Stoober with a bottle. And she's gone. They've both gone."

Porter turned his wide eyes to Dixon and Dixon laughed.

Chapter Twenty-Five

He stood up in his saddle, forgetting his discomfort for a moment, and waved to her. He grinned as she spurred her horse on, eager to be close to him once more.

They embraced without dismounting, White Dove leaning right over her horse's neck to grip him around the waist. They kissed and she looked into her eyes, smouldering as they were with happiness mixed with the sort of affection Noreen used to give him. He swallowed hard. "Anyone follow you?"

"There are men on the trail," she said, gesturing back the way she came with her fingers, "Four of them. They are maybe half a day behind."

Simms chewed at his lip. He grimaced as he eased himself back into his saddle, and touched his side where the bruising was at its worst. "Did you see who they were?"

She shook her head. "Soldiers maybe, I do not know. But whoever they are, they are in a hurry."

"Then we'd best be too. I don't want them to catch us out here in the open."

"We go to your town?"

"No." He saw her quizzical look and reached out to squeeze her arm. "There's a friend I know, a Kiowa by the name of Deep Water. He built himself a log cabin halfway between Glory and Bovey. He'll help."

"You have a Kiowa friend? You always surprise me."

He felt the heat spreading around his jaw line. "No, I'm not so much of a mystery, I promise. But out here, with no carbine and only one six-gun to help, we won't stand much of a chance against four men intent on running us down, so it's best we get to Deep Water and make a stand of sorts there."

"You think it will come to that?"

"I'm thinking that Porter would not have sent four men. He wouldn't have time to arrange it, and I'm guessing he wouldn't act so precipitously, not without Colonel Johnstone's say so. I reckon it's someone else. The ones who set me up in the first place."

"The men who murdered the soldier?"

"The very same. And their plan will almost certainly be to kill me out here, without witnesses. You too."

She did not flinch. "They must think you know something about them."

"A pity I don't – but we ain't in no position to get into a conversation with them. It'll be shoot first, ask later."

"So we ride."

"Through the night. You up to it?"

"Are you, after what they did?"

He smiled. "Hell, I've had worse than this. Besides, the bruises would only prevent me from sleeping anyway."

With his laughter ringing out, he turned his horse and spurred it into a gallop, with White Dove close behind, faces set straight ahead, determined.

They rode for as long as they were able, but when Simms very nearly fell from his saddle, White Dove insisted they stop and rest.

"We have to keep going," he said, his voice laced with exhaustion.

"No. The beating you took, it has taken away your strength. There is no choice. We rest for a few hours."

She did not make a fire to keep them warm in the night. She examined his body, running her finger tips over the swelling around his ribs and, using cold water only, gently washed them with a sodden rag. He moaned when she pressed too hard, but his discomfort soon gave way to a wonderful feeling of relaxation and security.

After she washed his face and cleaned the wounds around his eyes and mouth, she pulled two blankets over them both and huddled up next to him, wary not to squeeze too hard lest she brought another stab of pain. He put his arm around her and soon, despite his previous words, he drifted off to sleep.

The morning brought with it the promise of warmth, the sun already driving away any lingering clouds. They breakfasted on broken biscuits and some beef jerky White Dove found in her saddlebag. Then, they packed away and rode on. By the position of the sun in the sky, Simms calculated they had slept for a little over three hours. His limbs were sore, every bone calcified, every muscle stiff. She helped him up into the saddle and he looked at her with a pained expression.

"If we reach higher ground," she said, "we will be able to see how far away they are."

"Good idea." He nodded towards the soaring range around them. "If we can find a path, we will—"

"I know a path," she said, her voice flat. She ignored his frown and flicked the reins of her pony. "Follow my lead."

They made good progress along the ancient trail, climbing through jagged rocks punctuated with gnarled trees and clumps of sage, leaving the plain far behind them. White Dove traversed as if she knew every step, guiding her mount around crumbling promontories, hidden pitfalls and unstable ground. Simms, more than happy to give her the lead, studied her slim back, the material of her simple dress revealing every rippling muscle. He smiled ruefully to himself. He knew so little about this extraordinary woman, but what he knew brought him comfort and pride.

She reined in and twisted in around. "We leave the horses here and take a route to the top." She pointed to the summit of the rock. "From here the path skirts around to the far side, so we will not be able to see them from there. Can you climb?"

"I think so."

"If you cannot, you must say."

He grinned. "Let's just say I'll give it my best."

She slipped from her mount and lashed the reins around the roots of a sparse thicket. Extending her hand, she took his weight as he slipped from his saddle, both of them grunting as his feet hit the ground. They exchanged a smile before she tied his horse to her own.

Simms peered towards the summit and for a moment wavered, unsure if his strength would last. Pressing his tongue up against his top lip, he pulled in a deep breath and beckoned White Dove to ascend. Without a word, she did so, moving with all the purposefulness of a mountain goat. Simms followed with far more care, testing every handhold, easing up his legs, inching his way upwards. He paused every few moments, putting his forehead against the hard surface, giving his body time, waiting for the pain to drain from his limbs.

She made the summit long before him, squatting down to look out across the broad, open plains. As Simms struggled, straining to haul his body over the final overhang, she took him by the wrist and helped him over the lip. He fell on his face, breath coming in desperate gasps. His lungs were on fire, his throat parched, swallowing difficult. From somewhere, she pressed the open neck of her animal skin gourd to his lips and he took the first mouthful, violent coughing racking through him. Spluttering, he got up on his hands and knees, taking his time before he nodded and accepted another drink. This time he swallowed and, with no resulting cough, he looked at her, every fibre of his body screaming gratitude.

Keeping herself low, she moved across to the side of the promontory that afforded the best view. Simms scrambled alongside, shielding his eyes from the glare. "Wish I had my old German field-glasses with me. Can you see anything?"

"There is something," she said, but sounded unsure. "If we wait, we might have a better view."

"But if we wait too long …"

They exchanged a look, both realizing time was not their friend. "Whatever happens, I doubt they will come up here," she said. "The path is dangerous, and as they do not know the way, they could stumble and fall." Turning her face to the plain, she narrowed her eyes. "They will continue to follow the trail. We should wait here, allow them to pass us by, then head off to the north by a different route, towards the home of your friend."

"There's Utes across that way. If we're not careful, we might end up as food for their camp dogs."

"Then we wait. Another option is to fight them here."

"I have six bullets and there are maybe three, perhaps even four of them. That's not good odds."

"I have a knife."

"And they probably have two six-guns each, and carbines. If we keep going, follow the trail, we'll make it to the river. There's a ford I know of and we can cross it and make our way—"

Her hand shot out, gripping him by the forearm. Her neck strained, tendons rigid, chin jutting forward, body alert. "I see them."

Simms followed her gaze, but all he could make out was a tiny smudge on the horizon. As he looked, however, the shapes grew more distinct. Riders, their horses throwing up clouds of dust in their wake. He counted four. Not good odds, as he already predicted, but the knowledge brought no comfort. Instinctively, his hand fell to the revolver in his belt and he cursed himself for not taking the time to acquire more firearms.

"Look."

Her voice was low, edged with tension and surprise. Her slim fingers pointed way off to their left and Simms did his best to pick out what it was she saw. "What is it?"

"More riders. Many."

He shuffled forward on his belly, but all he made out was more dust. It could be a squall of wind, a fluctuation in the air. Anything. "I don't see them."

"*There*," she snapped, fingers thrust out.

And then he saw them, emerging from those clouds of dust. More than ten, perhaps more than twenty. And as they raced across the plain, the original group of four slowed and formed up into a tight semi-circle.

"Dear God," he whispered, terrified at what he saw. "Those others - they're Indians."

"They are our salvation," she said, unable to keep the joy from her voice; she rolled over to him and kissed him hard on the lips. When she drew her head backwards, she was grinning.

Chapter Twenty-Six

They galloped through the day and on into the night, through forests, fording streams and over the plain. Deep Water drove his pony on at a furious rate, pushing the animal to its limits until the morning came and then, spent, it collapsed and lay, chest heaving, unable to take another step. Taking her by the hand, he wasted no time in breaking into a run, Melody behind, crying out in terror, "They'll kill us."

If he heard her, he gave no reaction. With his head down, teeth clenched, he pressed on towards the rocks and tangled trees in the distance. He daren't pause, not even to check behind him. He knew full well Long Elk's companions would be closing in, full of bloodthirsty rage, their only desire to slice open his guts and drag out his entrails. What they would do to the woman was beyond imagining. So he ran on, his lungs on fire, his legs screaming, eyes clouded with sweat.

Melody stumbled more than once, hissing out in pain as her knees struck the hard earth. Before she could recover, he was already pulling her forward.

"We must make cover," he rasped. But his strength was not endless. Soon he would have to slow down, perhaps even halt, take in water. Every minute he did so, they would close in.

Then he heard them. They were not only behind, but ahead as well. He stopped, heart hammering, chest heaving, unable to believe such a thing could have occurred. How had they managed to get so far ahead? Despair fell over him, pushing him down to his knees. He checked his carbine and his revolvers. He would take as many of them as he could before they overwhelmed him, saving one bullet for the girl.

Snapping his head around, he saw her sitting in the dirt, gulping in breath, hair bedraggled, hanging like slick, heavy ropes over her face. "There may only be a few," he said, knowing his words sounded hollow. She turned up her face, her eyes wet with tears.

"You should have left me there."

"I could not. I saw you and I knew I had no choice but to help you."

"But you were their friend."

"No. I traded with them, giving them iron pots, knives and axes for cured buffalo skins, moccasins, anything I could sell. I was never their friend."

"But you are *one* of them."

He shook his head and looked again at the approaching group of riders. Something in the way they rode made him sit up and reconsider his initial thoughts.

They were not Indians.

They were white men. Four of them, riding with an easy gait, tall in the saddle, faces and clothes covered in dust. As they drew closer, he wondered who they were and what their purpose was, riding out in this dangerous place. He sighed and climbed to his feet, carbine cradled across his chest. Without turning he said, "Remain still. There are four. If need be, I shall kill them and we will take their horses."

"Oh God," she muttered.

"Stay still."

So she did. And Deep Water too, waiting, controlling his breathing, watching them draw closer.

Some dozen or so paces away, the men reined in their snorting horses and they sat and considered these two strange people who ran across open ground like deer pursued by a pack of wolves.

"Good day to you, friend," said the lead man, a huge individual with a broad, red, freckled face, a Derby hat perched at a jaunty angle on his ginger-topped head. He wore thickly padded clothes made from animal skins, turned grey with sweat and grime. Around his ample middle he wore a gun belt, holster tied down, and a revolver, its walnut grip worn smooth with ample use. He grinned, twisted his lips and spat into the ground. "Might you be off on a little walk in the country?"

His companions cackled at this, one of them whooping so loud his laughter carried right across the prairie, no doubt reaching the ears of those who pursed Deep Water.

"Our horse died," Deep Water said evenly, his gaze settling on the lead rider. "We have little water and no food."

"Then that makes you kinda dumb, don't it?" spoke up another rider, kicking his horse's flank to come up alongside the big man. "You seen anyone out here?"

Deep Water blinked, "Anyone? You mean—"

"I mean a couple, a man and a squaw. The exact opposite of yourself."

"Strange you should be out here," said the big man, "a Redskin and a White woman."

"You steal her?"

"Did he steal you, honey?"

Deep Water shot a glance to Melody, who got to her feet and stepped up close to her Indian saviour. "I am with him by my own free will."

"Well, well," said the big man, twisting to grin at his companions, "did you hear that, boys? Her own free will."

"You must have seen someone else," continued the second man, not joining in with the jokes. "Out here, all alone, not seeing anyone, I find that kinda hard to swallow. You could be in cahoots with this fella."

"I know of no *fella.*"

"Man's name is Simms," said the big one, leaning forward in his saddle. "He's a killer, broke out of jail yesterday and is making his way over to a town called Glory."

"Bovey is what I understand," said the other man.

Derby Hat shrugged, sighed and spat. "Well, wherever he's headin', we'll find him. We aim to take him back and hang him for what he done."

Deep Water's gaze remained impassive. "I know of no such man."

"So how come you is out here?"

"I told you. We were riding and—"

"No one rides out here alone, bub. You stole this girl, didn't you? You stole her and you're making a run for it."

"That is not true."

"I believe it is." He deftly brought out his revolver, snapping back the hammer. "Now, honey, you tell your Uncle Liam the truth, you hear. This black-eyed bastard won't harm you, not anymore."

Melody clung onto Deep Water's arm. "He did not steal me."

"You mean, you are his woman?" the second rider said, gawping in disbelief. "What in the hell, are you missing some screws in that pretty head of yours? He's a goddamned savage."

"Hey Brad," piped up one of the others from behind, "I think we have company."

Every eye turned to look out towards the distant horizon, from where a great cloud of dust developed.

"What in the hell?" said Derby Hat, who called himself Liam.

"They friends of yours?" asked Brad, bringing out his own revolver.

"No," said Deep Water flatly. "They are here to kill us." He looked at each rider in turn. "All of us."

"They Indians?"

"Shoshone. I helped this woman to escape from them. They want her back."

"Holy Saint Francis," said Liam and spat in to the earth again, "then we'll just have to give you back, won't we."

"You can't," yelped Melody, stepping away from Deep Water, hands struck out, imploring. "Mercy. They'll kill me – they'll kill us all."

"No they won't," said Liam. "I reckon they'll be mighty pleased to have you back."

"No," said Deep Water, "she speaks true. They will kill us all."

"You kinda stupid, ain't you," said Brad, leering, "telling us all this, knowing we'll do what we need to do."

"I told you because together we can beat them." He held up his carbine. "I am good with this. Better than most."

"Holy Mother," said one of the others, "I count twenty. Could be more. Liam, we better get to cover."

Grunting, Liam looked over to Brad, "I reckon we shouldn't take the chance. Best we make a stand here, kill or drive 'em off, then sort out this other little problem afterwards."

"I reckon you could be right," said Brad.

Liam put away his revolver, "Honey, you get up behind me, and you, you black-eyed bastard, you run. Make for those rocks," he pointed to an area where the land ran into a small dip, circled by outcrops of rock of various size.

Melody whimpered something and Deep Water took her hand and led her over to Liam, who reached out and lifted her onto his horse's back with ease. He flicked his reins across the animal's neck and swung her around. He let out a high-pitched cry and kicked the animal into a gallop, pounding off across the earth towards the dip. The others followed, Brad remaining for a moment, one eyebrow arched, studying Deep Water. "If you're lying about all of this—"

"I'm not lying."

"Then you'd better run, boy, 'cause they are cutting up a tidy trail." Then he too was gone, beating his horse's rump with his hat.

Deep Water let out a long sigh, calculating the distance to the dip and that to the approaching Shoshone warband. He didn't give much for his chances but set off with a loping gait towards where the others were already dismounting.

He hoped he could make it.

Chapter Twenty-Seven

The town was busier than usual. A train of settlers milled about outside one of the two merchant stores, filling up their wagons with a host of supplies. Children played on the street, indulging in a game of tag, squealing with excitement as they darted in and out between the wheels and the horses. Men strained to load the wagons with heavy bags of grain, flour and bales of hay, together with farm tools and several old muskets. They all stopped as Dodd came riding in, astride his horse with the mule plodding behind, not seeming to care for its own burden of two bodies draped over its back.

Silas came out of his office, answering the hectic yells from his deputy to raise himself. He stood in his long johns, strapping on his gun belt, and gaped as the gunfighter drew up to the hitching rail and tied up his mount.

"I reckon these bastards could be worth a hundred, maybe even two after what they did." Dodd eased himself down from of his saddle, stretched and took to rubbing his behind.

"What in the name of dear God Almighty have you done?"

"Don't be coming on all sanctimonious now, Sheriff," said Dodd, stepping up onto the boardwalk. "You would have done the same."

"They were to go on trial, you hothead." The deputy beside him grumbled. Silas shot him a vicious look. "Keep your comments to yourself, Vaughn."

Chuckling, Dodd said, "Well, they would have ended up dead, either way. At least now I can claim the reward."

"We ain't got no papers on 'em," said the deputy.

Dodd levelled his gaze towards the young man. "I think you should check on that, son."

The deputy went to take a step forward, but Silas threw out his arm to bar the way. "Easy, Vaughn. You just do as the man says."

"Damned if I will, Silas. This man is no better than they is."

"*Were*," corrected Dodd with a smile. "Now, you do as the good sheriff says, son. I'll wait."

Grumbling, the young deputy disappeared inside. Silas looked to the street, beyond Dodd and the gathering of settlers, all showing great interest in Dodd and his grizzly cargo. "Folks, you go on back to whatever it is you're doing. This ain't no circus." He turned his eye on the gunfighter. "I knew you were trouble the moment I saw you."

"I did you a good deed, Sheriff, even though you can't admit it. These boys were killers. They killed poor old Dan and that entire family and—"

"You can't possibly know that!"

"Yes I can – because one of them told me before he died. They would have taken out your sorry bunch of deputies in a breath. From where I'm standing, I think I saved quite a few mothers in this town from burying their boys."

"You are one arrogant bastard, mister."

"Save your sermons and just give me the money I'm due. Then I'll be taking a visit to the assayer's office. I have a claim to amend."

"What in the hell are you talking about?"

"I'm talking about my old friend Dan Stoakes. He made a claim, and these sons-of-botches took it from him."

"So they really did kill him?"

"Have you got shit in your ears, Sheriff? I just told you – but where they put the body I have not yet been able to ascertain. Perhaps after I have made myself more comfortable, I shall return to the mine and explore further."

"Made yourself more comfortable? What in the hell does that mean?"

"It means I have some unfinished business to attend to over at Ritter's eating place. Then I might buy it, together with the saloon. Settle down."

"You can't – I won't allow it."

Dodd smiled and tapped Silas on the chest. "Pipe down and unruffle your feathers, you old cockerel. I'm here to stay and there ain't a damned thing you can do about it. Unless, of course, you'd like to try?"

For a prolonged moment they both stood, within inches of one another, the only sound that of the sheriff's heavy breathing. He jumped when the office door creaked open and Vaughn reappeared. "I can't find no papers," he said, before sensing the charged atmosphere. "What the hell is this?"

"Just a few details that needed ironing out," said Dodd and stepped away. "Son, you wire the details of these boys over to Laramie, check if they have any papers on 'em there."

"We asked for a marshal to come, out of Bridger. Maybe he has something."

"All right then, wire him again. I want my reward." He tipped his hat and clumped down the steps to his horse. "Oh, the mule is mine too. I'd be grateful if, after you've taken these sacks of shit over to the undertakers, you'd give him some oats and a good brush down. Obliged to you."

Dodd dipped into his waistcoat pocket and flicked a coin across to the young deputy who snatched at it and, instinctively, bit down to test its authenticity. He nodded. "Seems fair."

"It is," said Dodd and narrowed his eyes towards Silas. "Let us hope, for your sake, you too are fair, Sheriff."

Stepping up next to the Sheriff, Vaughn sighed. "That is one scary individual, Silas. I hope you ain't fixing on confronting him."

Silas ran his tongue over his teeth, hawked and spat. "Shut you mouth. I'll do what I need to do."

"I reckon you need to think long on that. Strikes me he is a man well versed in killing." He brushed past the sheriff and stepped down onto the street. He went over to the mule and checked the bodies. Shaking his head, he turned again to gaze at Silas. "We should let it be. He ain't done nothing, has he? Broken no laws, I mean."

But Silas wasn't listening. He stood watching Dodd slowly ride off down the street towards Ritter's, whilst his stomach rolled over, grew slack and his throat closed up. There was wisdom in the young deputy's words, words which he should take note of, but the more he watched the gunfighter's back the more he realised there was a reckoning coming and there was nothing he could do to stop it.

Chapter Twenty-Eight

From their vantage point, Simms and White Dove watched the skirmish below. The Shoshone warriors peeled off in two groups, sweeping out in wide arcs to surround their quarry in a sort of pincer movement. Puffs of smoke bloomed, followed by the sharp crack of gunfire moments later. But it proved impossible to make out if anyone fell, the figures like ants.

White Dove said, "I thought I saw two others joining them. Without horses."

"I didn't see. That would make six of them all told. Not good odds, not the way those Shoshone are going at it."

"They might think it is us."

"I was thinking much the same."

"Then we take the chance and we get away."

Simms mulled this over, sucking at his teeth, locked in an inner struggle. "Whoever comes out of it will still come looking for us."

"Yes, but by the time they realise, we will be gone."

"So you're thinking those Shoshone will prevail?"

Her face creased into something reminiscent of a smile. "I have no doubt."

"You sound as if you know for certain."

"Maybe I do."

And with that, she rolled away, tugging at his arm. With distant gunfire echoing across the prairie, they scrambled down the way they came, to their horses and the chance for escape.

* * *

Deep Water ran, legs and arms pumping, his lungs fit to burst, but no matter how much effort he put in, the dip seemed to be forever distant. He needed to stop, to recover, to conquer the sharp stabs of pain breaking out across his ribs and in his gut. Wincing, sweat dripping into his eyes, he slowed and stood bent double, panting. Behind him, the pounding of hooves came ever nearer. He turned and saw them, splitting off into long arms, one going left, the other right. As they separated, two warriors spotted him standing still and, whooping loudly, they struck out and charged towards him. Dragging a shaking hand across his brow, he dropped to one knee and brought his carbine up to his shoulder and squinted along the barrel. He held his breath, stilling his heart, settling his aim. And he waited.

On they came, one slightly ahead, a wicked looking spear held aloft. Deep Water honed in on the man's wild eyes, eyes filled with venom and hatred, oblivious to danger, intent only on killing.

Deep Water waited. A few more paces. He could almost smell the warrior's sweat.

He shot him in the chest, the heavy calibre bullet lifting the Shoshone into the air and throwing him off his horse, dumping him some half dozen paces to the rear. His companion continued for a moment or two before pulling the reins back hard, the pony screaming in outrage, rearing up, confused, terrified. The warrior struggled with his bow, nocking an arrow to the string whilst trying unsuccessfully to keep his mount still. It whirled, stamped and fought to break free; all the while Deep Water was running, running straight towards the Shoshone, his own war cry splitting the heavy air, rushing up to him, brandishing the carbine like a club and smashing him across the midriff with all of his strength.

The warrior fell to the earth; his pony, free from any constraints, pounded away as Deep Water fell on his enemy and drove his knife the blade deep into the fallen man's throat.

Sweeping up the bow and the quiver, Deep Water retreated to the dip, the whooping of war cries close. He ran hard, head down, not daring to look back. As he approached the hollow in the ground, he found the men were already discharging their weapons, wild, futile, hopeless efforts, the baying Shoshones wheeling in a caracole, moving close to loose arrows before turning away. None paid Deep Water much mind until one of them took aim and put an arrow in the back of his thigh.

He fell face down into the dirt and lay there in disbelief. He craned his neck. No more than ten paces separated him from the men. He thought he caught a glimpse of Melody's head, but he could not be sure. Another arrow thudded into the ground, inches from his head and he struggled to wriggle forward.

The pain struck him like a searing, hot knife blade, penetrating deep into the muscle. He screeched, clutching at the protruding dart. It was embedded in the flesh by two inches or more and he knew instinctively he could not pull it out. Not yet, not there. Another arrow singing overhead emphasised the point and he gritted his teeth, gripped the shaft and broke the arrow a little more than six inches from the tip. He screamed, writhing over onto his back and then, from somewhere, a strong hand had him by the shoulder and was dragging him across the impacted earth. e looked up and recongised He looked up and recognised Brad. The shock almost made him squawk.

"Come on, you redskinned-son-of-a-bitch, we need you."

Surrendering to the man's strength, Deep Water allowed himself to be dragged like a piece of meat across to the dip. At the lip, Brad pushed him over, rolling him down to where Melody waited, crying with relief when she saw him.

Brad made to get down beside them. An arrow hit him in the neck and he stood, eyes wide with amazement. Another hit home between his shoulders and he fell to his knees.

"Brad!" came a voice.

One of the others broke cover, fanning his revolver, scrambling over the slight incline to his friend who knelt there, unblinking, bewildered, a trail of blood running from the corner of his mouth.

"Billy, is that you?"

"Oh sweet Jesus," said the other, dropping down next to his friend, holding him about the shoulder. "No, Brad, no. Come on, we have—"

His words were cut off as an arrow sank into his chest and he pitched backwards, his gun falling from his cold, lifeless hands. And all the while Brad remained on his knees, his mouth moving, blood dripping down onto his vest.

Deep Water waved Melody away, whipping out his revolver, and stood up. Ignoring the pain, concentrating on the Indians circling closer, he fired measured shots, felling two more warriors from the six bullets he fired. Without pausing, he pulled out his second revolver and repeated the action. One more Shoshone hit the earth.

"Dear God," said Liam above the screams and the bullets, shuffling forward towards Brad. He took him by the front of his torn and tattered shirt and hauled him down into the dip. Mindful of the protruding arrow in his friend's back, he gently eased him onto his side and went rigid.

Brad was dead.

Moving over to them both, Deep Water pulled out Brad's revolver from its holster and loosed off two more shots. He snapped his head towards Liam. "The other group, they are moving to the rear. They mean to surround us. Have you a rifle?"

Dumbstruck, Liam merely looked down at his dead friend. Deep Water shook him by the shoulders and a sudden light flicked on in his eyes. "Rifle? Yes, yes, over at my horse."

"We need powder and shot. I lost my carbine out there, so we have nothing but the revolvers. I will do my best to—"

"I'll do the reloading," said Melody, coming up beside him. "You two carry on firing, I'll load up the guns."

Deep Water smiled then shot a glance at their last, remaining companion, some paces away, doing his very best with his own revolver. "His name?"

"Jonas. Jonas Meeps."

Deep Water hobbled over to the young man frantically trying to reload his piece, noted how his hands shook like material whipped up by the wind, and gently relieved him of the gun, exchanging it for Brad's. "Here, take this. Melody will reload. You watch the rear of the dip. They will come that way soon. You have four shots in this gun. Make them count."

Jonas gave a feeble nod then Deep Water limped across to the horses and pulled out one of the rifles. It was an ancient weapon, but was loaded and primed. He took out what powder and shot there was from the saddlebags.

The dip was little more than twenty paces across at its widest point, with scant cover at its base. The lip afforded reasonable protection from arrows and spears, but once the Indians were inside, the fight would be swift, bloody and final. With no room to retreat, Deep Water knew there was little hope. His plan was to take as many of them down as he could before the inevitable conclusion. As before, he made the grim decision to save his last bullet for Melody, who faced an unthinkable fate at the hands of those wild, blood-crazed warriors.

Simms was breathing hard when he finally managed to drop down to where the horses were tethered. White Dove was well ahead of him. She reached out to untie her horse when the first warrior loomed up, gripping her around the neck, pulling her to him as his knife flashed in the sunlight.

Going into a crouch, Simms brought up his gun in a blur and shot the warrior in the head. He fell back and White Dove screamed and dropped to her knees. For a terrible moment, the detective believed he had shot her by mistake, but when he took a step closer he realised this was not the case.

From out of the clumps of sage and withered trees, the second warrior sprang with all the grace and agility of a puma, his hard, naked body slamming into him with terrific force. They crashed to the ground, the air blasting out of Simms's lungs. He fought like someone possessed, hands flailing about, trying to parry and block the blows raining down upon him, but the warrior proved too strong and soon he had Simms pinned, his knees pressing down on the detective's arms. He reared back, laughing maniacally. Soon, it would be over.

White Dove struck the warrior in the back of his head with a fallen branch she found. She swung the piece of wood with such force it shattered across the man's skull and he crumpled onto his side, groaning, his hatchet slipping from numbed fingers.

Simms rolled over, put the muzzle of his gun into the man's temple and fired.

White Dove screamed again.

The first Shoshone jumping into the dip received a bullet from Deep Water's rifle and fell. Melody handed the Scout a revolver and he worked at the hammer, shooting two more warriors as they came screaming over the top.

"They're backing off," shouted Liam from the other side, firing off shots from his own gun, keeping his aim steady. "I counted six down. They're losing the thirst for it."

Grunting, Deep Water kept his eyes on the opposite edge of the dip, knowing they would come. Melody handed over another revolver. "You've got eight shots. There are no more."

He snapped his head towards her. "Then we are lost."

"No," she said, reaching out to take his hand. "We've come this far, we ain't going to lose it all now."

They came then, in a single line, dismounted, whooping out their war cries. Eight of them, moving like flashes of light, swift, focused and determined. They held hatchets and knives, two of them loosing arrows but moving too quickly to be certain of their aim. Sprinting, keeping low, darting from side to side.

The others came and stood alongside Deep Water. After exchanging a quick glance, they brought up their firearms. Their guns bucked and barked, spitting out death in a thunderous volley, followed swiftly by another, then another. Not one of the warriors made it close enough to put weapons into flesh. They fell, wounded and dying, with the three survivors lopping away, back over the lip, disappearing out of sight.

Clouds of black powder smoke clung in the still air, the memories of the blasts drifting out across the open land. They stood, taking in gulps of air, not daring to believe it might be over.

But, of course, it was not.

The second attack came from the rear. The Shoshone were not defeated, not yet, and they sprang upon their unsuspecting enemies, wild cats pouncing on their prey.

Melody screamed, backing away as the men fought against this new assault. Perhaps five Shoshone warriors overwhelmed Liam and his companion whilst Deep Water swept up the rifle, wielding it like a warrior of old, sending it around in a wide arc to crack against the skull of his first assailant.

Over to his right, more warriors fought with the two men. Two of them took apart young Jonas, one skewering him through the neck with a spear, whilst the second sank his blade deep into his gut, ripping the knife upwards to the breastbone, spilling out a great oily mess of intestines. They severed his head and held it aloft, screeching high-pitched, triumphant.

Liam worked his revolver, despite it being empty, and the other Shoshone fell over him. His strength saved him, at least at first. His right fist cracked into the first warrior, an elbow putting paid to the second. As he turned to unleash another punch, the third warrior brandished his hatchet and brought it down in a vicious swipe to slice through his arm. The big Irishman screamed, clutching at the blood spurting from his half-severed limb. A second warrior leaped onto his back, the blade sinking into the big man's side. Impossibly, he swung the Shoshone over his shoulder and dumped him on the ground, kicking him across the jaw. Another he back-handed to the dirt, preparing to punch him again when the third, like a spirit, swift, invisible, plunged a knife into Liam again. He gave a great groan, clinging onto the assailant, and fell down with a loud, solid thump. A hand closed around his throat, the blade sawing through the top of his skull, to scalp him before he breathed his last.

A gunshot rang out, blowing the warrior to the side.

Deep Water looked up in the direction of the blast, still holding the rifle by the barrel, ready to swing again.

He saw him, looming over the ridge, the revolver held low, the hammer falling, shooting one more Shoshone through the throat before the remainder broke and ran, blood still dripping from their hands.

"Oh dear God," screamed Melody, clamping both hands over her mouth. Deep Water hobbled over and pulled her to him, holding her tight.

"It is all right," he said, the rifle sliding from his hand, his voice shaking with the shock and strain of the struggle. "It is all all right now."

Simms stepped forward and looked his old friend deep in the eyes. And then they embraced.

Chapter Twenty-Nine

Dixon packed his few things in a bedroll and paused for a moment to look along the barrack room. The twin line of bunks, on either side of a narrow passageway, were all empty. Few soldiers billeted there and now, in the cold of the morning, it seemed a lonely and forlorn place. He shuddered despite himself and went out, unable to shrug off the feeling of gloom settling over him.

Outside, the square rang with the everyday bustle he had come to accept. Trappers, traders, pioneers, trudged through on foot, rode astride mangy-looking mules, or guided clapped-out wagons towards the over-burdened merchant store. Fort Bridger was the last place of safety for two days, until the trail reached Glory, and nobody wanted to take anything for granted traversing the open plain. Stories of Indians and cutthroats filled the tightly-packed confines of Clancy's and, for those from the east especially, the whole area seemed like the very essence of the wild frontier.

A sudden burst of noise, raised voices, the yells of uniformed sergeants, brought him to a halt. He stood on the narrow boardwalk outside the barracks and stared across to the wide open gates through which a dust-spattered group of tired and hungry-looking soldiers threaded their way. At their head was a straight-backed officer, his wide brimmed straw hat casting his face in shadow. Nevertheless, Dixon knew who it was. Colonel Johnstone, the gruff, no-nonsense commander of the fort.

What took most of Dixon's attention, however, was the much smaller man riding alongside the Colonel, dressed in well-tailored tweeds.

Kieran Danks, stagecoach owner and the man Dixon knew was trying to swindle him out of his share in the company. The wily old bastard had outflanked him, no doubt, soliciting the Colonel's aid in any altercation which may follow.

As he caught Danks' surprised look, Dixon's legs buckled from under him, forcing him to reach out with an outstretched palm to support himself against the nearby barrack wall. He swallowed hard, knowing the cards were now heavily stacked against him.

Tabatha rolled off him and lay down, staring up at the ceiling, bare-breasted, murmuring softly. "My, how I missed you."

He sniggered and propped himself up on one elbow. Dodd licked his index finger and rotated it around the closest nipple. She arched her back, eyes squeezed shut, and reached out for him, urging him closer. He obliged and settled his lips around her breast, seeking her out with his tongue. She clawed at his hair and then cried out in frustration as he suddenly slipped out from beneath the bed sheet and stood up.

"What you doing?"

"I have to get ready," he said, pulling on his shirt.

"Ready? Ready for what?"

"I have to go over to the bank, deposit my reward. I can't take the chance of leaving such a sum lying around in my saddle-bags."

"Do you have to go now? I was hoping we could spend the afternoon together."

He smiled and sat down beside her. She put her head in his lap and he ran his fingers through her hair. "We'll have all the time in the world to stay together."

"You mean it?"

"Of course I mean it. I have no need to go anywhere else, not now. I have the money and, together with Dan's claim, I'll have enough collateral to buy this place and the saloon."

"You seriously want to buy this place?"

"Why not? Set you up as manageress – I reckon you could make a success of it. I'd like to develop the saloon, turn it into a better class of hotel. People are still making their way out west, Tabby; if we can offer them the sort of place that will give them a decent night's rest and a fine meal, word will soon get out."

"We?" She frowned. "You said 'we'."

He smiled and kissed the top of her head. "Well of course. That's what I want. You and me. Together."

She felt her eyes growing wet. "Dear God, you really mean it?"

He laughed and she threw her arms around him, the tears coming unchecked. He smoothed down her hair, kissing the top of her head again. "Don't fret none, Tabby. You must have known. Ever since I first lay eyes on you, I couldn't help myself."

"I never dared believe it might be true."

"Hush. You just think about all that's gonna happen. We have the chance of a future, you and me. A real future."

"But Silas," she said, sniffing, pulling her face back. "Silas isn't going to let you do all those things. He won't stop until he finds a reason to run you out of town."

"Yeah, well ... " He leaned over and kissed her before standing up again. He pulled on his trousers, tucked in his shirt and flopped down on the edge of the bed to pull on his boots. "I reckon Silas and I will need to lay to rest some of our differences."

"You be careful of him. He's mean and untrustworthy."

"Darlin', don't you go worrying about me. The sheriff and I have an understanding." He winked, "He understands I'll kill him if he gets in my way."

She put her arms around him again. "God, you are so strong, so brave. I feel so safe with you and I wish to God I'd known you before."

"Before? Before what?"

"Oh, just what I told you. How it used to be, with my mother."

"Out on the range?" He turned and raised her chin. "Darlin', all of that is well behind you now. I understand that the loss of you mother is a painful one, but you have to—"

"No, it's not that. It's …" Lowering her eyes, she dabbed a handkerchief she kept under the pillow at a new sprouting of tears rolling down her cheek. "It's of no matter."

"Yes, it is. What's eating away at you? The grief?"

"Yes, that and who was responsible – who *is* responsible. I don't think I'll ever know peace until he is lying six feet under."

"You mean you actually know who it is who killed your mother? I don't understand. I thought it was fever or something."

"Oh dear God, if only it were. No, it wasn't any type of fever, unless you can call that murderous bastard's bullets a fever. A sickness. Of the mind."

Taking hold of her shoulders, he stared at her, his eyes narrowing, concerned. "Tell me."

"I don't think I should. It's my problem; one which I have to live with, I guess."

"I told you – we're together now. So you tell me who it was and I'll end all of this suffering for you."

"I couldn't ask you to do such a thing. It wouldn't be right."

"Nonsense. You mean everything to me, Tabby. I've travelled across every goddamned square inch of this territory and you're the first decent thing I've found in all that time. So tell me who it is."

"His name is Simms, and he lives in Glory."

Standing behind his desk, Johnstone read through the hastily scribbled report Thorpe presented to him within fifteen minutes of the Colonel's return. "You seriously expect me to believe this, Major?"

Thorpe squirmed under his commanding officer's penetrating glare and shot a glance towards Dixon, who merely shrugged. "I did initially, sir. I understand now that my initial suspicions were a mistake."

"And the killers of this man? The *real* killers?"

Dixon coughed. In the corner sat Danks, face a perfect mask of fury. "I believe I can answer that question, Colonel. I have made some investigations and *my* suspicions have fallen upon a scoundrel by the name of O'Shaughnessy."

"Dear God," spat Danks, leaping to his feet before Johnstone could make further comment. "That fetid Irishman who burned down my stage?"

"The very same. He tried to befriend me and I played him along – knowing the sort of murderous villain he is." He caught Danks' quizzical look. "I'm a lawman as well, you know. My profession equips me to know these things. O'Shaughnessy did not know this, of course. If he had, he may well have tried to kill me. Instead, he framed Simms, knowing full well, being a Pinkerton, his keen skill in investigating would have revealed the treacherous plan the Irishman had in mind."

"And when Simms escaped, the Irishmen went after him." Johnstone put down the papers and folded his arms. "What do you think his plan is if he succeeds in this endeavour?"

Dixon shrugged. "Return here, kill me; you too, Kieran, once he discovered you were here. None of us would be safe. However," he smiled a thin oily smile, humourless, uncomfortable to see, "I do not see him succeeding. Detective Simms is a man of considerable means. In a gunfight, I doubt there are many who are his measure."

"So what do you propose?" asked Danks.

"Firstly, I must travel to Twin Buttes. They have requested I go there to apprehend certain criminals. We could go together, Kieran; that way we can either confront O'Shaughnessy on the way, or talk to Simms over in Glory after my business in Twin Buttes is concluded."

"Sounds like a plan," said Johnstone.

Danks chewed at his bottom lip for a moment. "Yes. I see the logic in it. Perhaps we could visit the site of my proposed staging post."

"Then we shall leave directly," said Dixon and turned to leave.

"Hold on Marshall," said Johnstone quickly. "I shall order two men to go with you. Good men, who know the country."

Dixon paused with his fingers on the door handle. He looked back, face a blank. "That will not be necessary, Colonel, I assure you."

"It's no trouble," said Johnstone with a smile. "Besides, Mr Danks is tired. We picked him up on this side of the Colorado River and we have been in the saddle ever since. After a good night's rest, you can set out at first light."

Dixon remained impassive, breathing steady, shoulders relaxed. "Very well. Until tomorrow morning."

He went out, closing the door behind him and only then did he lean back, close his eyes and silently curse the world and everything in it.

Chapter Thirty

Dodd took breakfast in the bar, nodding his thanks as the barman brought him over more coffee and an extra slice of ham.

"I heard what you did."

Pausing in the act of putting a piece of bread into his mouth, Dodd peered at the man from under his brows. "What was it you heard I did?"

"Killing those two miserable bastards. The ones who murdered that family. It was the best thing that's happened around here for a good while."

Grunting, Dodd munched down the bread, took a sip of the coffee and leaned back in his chair. He cleaned his mouth with a serviette. "Do you happen to know how far a town called Glory is from here?"

"Glory?"

Dodd frowned, noting the change in the man's demeanour. "That's right. Is there something wrong with it?"

"You could say that. Mind if I sit down?"

Another grunt and Dodd gestured for the barman to do so.

"If you ain't gonna finish that ham, then I would gladly—"

"Help yourself."

The man grinned, pulled Dodd's plate towards himself and attacked the ham with gusto. As he chewed down the meat, the juices running out the side of his mouth, he continued, "It's a hellish place. Least it was. A bunch of killers took it over, so the story goes. They strung up the mayor from a telegraph pole. Did you ever hear the like?"

"Not recently."

"Well, they did that and worse. By the time they finished, almost every person of any importance and influence was in the ground, 'cepting for some woman councillor who fell for the leader. She got hers in the end, like they all did."

"And how did that happen?"

"Well, I ain't exactly sure of the details."

"Take a wild guess."

The barman frowned for a moment, then resumed his tale, punctuated by mouthfuls of ham poked into his mouth with Dodd's fork. "Well, from what I know, this fella came into town and shot 'em all."

"Fella? What *fella*?"

"Lawman, out of Chicago, so they say."

"That's a long way. What was he doing in Glory?"

"I don't know. Something to do with some woman. Isn't it always?"

Dodd thought of Tabatha and gave a rueful smile. "Almost always."

"Anyways, this fella, he was what they call a Pinkerton Detective."

"I've heard of them."

"Yes, me too. At least, I have now seeing as this fella, this detective, he was the one who put them in the ground."

"He must be quite a man."

"He's quite a gunfighter, so the stories go. Can't think of his name."

"Can't be that famous then."

"Oh, he is, but my brain ... " To give credence to his words, he pounded his forehead with his fist. "Damn it all, it's in here somewhere."

"His name is Simms."

Both men looked up to see Tabatha standing there, dressed in a tight black waistcoat and billowing skirt.

"Hot dang, I do believe you is right," cried the barman and giggled. "Yes sir, that's it – Simms. He killed 'em all, he did."

Dodd, with his eyes glued on Tabatha, threw down his serviette and stood up. "Well, seems like everything is falling into place."

"I'm coming with you," she said.

"No."

"But you'll need me – you have no idea the type of man he is."

"I'm not sure you know what type of man I am."

"I believe you are a match for that callous son-of-a-bitch, but even so …"

"Even so, I go alone."

She stepped up to him and gripped his shirt front. The smell of her perfume invaded his nostrils and he closed his eyes for a moment, giddy with desire. She grinned. "What if I just tag along anyhow? You'll be in need of company out on that prairie, especially at night, with the sky so big and the air so cold. I'd keep you warm."

"Damn you, Tabby…"

She leaned into him and kissed him. "I'll get my coat."

She moved off and Dodd readjusted his shirt. As he reached out to pick up the coffee cup with its final mouthful waiting to be drunk, he noticed the barman looking at him, one eyebrow raised. "What?"

The man shrugged, "Oh, nothing. Like you said, there's almost always a lady involved." He giggled and stood up. "Somewhere."

Smiling, the man went to move away. Dodd reached out and touched him by the arm. "I have a proposition for you."

Pausing, the man's expression changed, a deep frown developing, eyes narrowing. "Has it anything to do with money?"

"I think that could form a substantial part of it. I want to pick your brains. I need some men. No more than three. I have some business to attend to over at Glory and I need some assistance."

"What sort of business?"

"The kind I'm willing to pay for. Fifty dollars per man – if they're good enough."

Intrigued, the barman turned back to Dodd's table and sat down opposite him. "Good enough for what, mister?"

Taking a quick look around the bar room, Dodd leaned forward, voice dropping to almost a whisper. "There may be some shooting and I need men who ain't afraid to step up, who will not spook at the first sound of gunfire."

Chewing his lip thoughtfully, the man leaned back in his chair, arms folding across his chest. "Men who are good with guns."

"Experienced men."

"I think I know a couple of boys. For fifty dollars apiece they'll be more than willing to lend a hand."

"Are they good?"

"The Stebbing brothers, Art and Sean. Art is the older one, a little more level-headed than his younger brother."

"Are they good, I asked?"

"Oh yes, they're good all right. Art was in the army, got thrown out after he killed a sergeant-major in a bar brawl. Only reason they didn't hang him was because the sergeant threw the first punch. Sean – hell, he is just plain loco. He's a dead-eye with a gun, though. Can't say I've seen anyone better, 'cepting one."

"And who might that be?"

The man beamed. "Me."

Smiling, Dodd thrust out his hand, "Then I have my three men, if you're willing to tag along."

"I am," the man replied, not offering his hand, "only not for a measly fifty dollars. If this *business* you is talking about involves gunplay, then I'll want a hundred, straight up."

Dodd considered his own outthrust hand. "You'd better be worth it."

"I am. I'll keep those two brothers in line, too. They can be something of a handful if they have a mind."

"They'd best save all of that for when we reach Glory." He thrust his hand out a little further. "You have a deal."

Smiling, the man shook Dodd's hand. "My name's Proctor. Elijah Proctor, but no one bothers with my first name no more."

"We meet over at the livery. Give it two hours. You think you can arrange things by then?"

"You're in one helluva hurry, mister."

"I am meaning to get this business sorted within two days. I ain't got time to tarry."

"Then I'll arrange it."

"You tell them boys, if all goes well, I'll double their pay – yours too."

Proctor's eyes widened. "I'm liking the sound of this deal more by the minute."

"Then clean your bar and get yourself set."

Shoving his chair back, Proctor strode over to the counter, Dodd watching the man's broad back. He never liked hiring gunhands he didn't know, but the situation demanded it. Nevertheless, he needed to continue with a fair degree of caution; if things turned somewhat sour, Simms would not be the only one falling down dead by the time everything was finished.

A little over two hours later, as he stood outside his office, Silas observed the silent group of riders easing their horses along the main street, Dodd in the lead, with the Stebbing brothers and Proctor behind. Bringing up the rear came Tabatha, muffled up to her ears in a thick coat. None showed any interest in the sheriff, so he coughed loudly and called out, "We have business to attend to, Dodd. Unfinished business."

"It'll keep," said the gunfighter without turning. "As soon as I'm back, everything will be sorted out just fine and dandy."

"I hope you're not planning on getting yourself killed, Dodd."

The only reply was the sound of chuckling and then they were out of earshot, a fact which did not stop Silas from staring at them as they disappeared into the distance.

"You think he'll come back?"

Silas shot a quick glance to Vince, standing in the doorway to the office. "Maybe, maybe not. I'm not sure I like the fact he's got himself tied up with those Stebbing boys."

"They're mean bastards, that's for sure. Proctor too. I've seen him crack a few heads before now."

Silas grunted. "I'm not sure it's cracking heads they'll be doing."

"Gunplay, more than likely."

"That woman, she seems to have a hold on Dodd, but for what reason I don't know. Listen, I want you to send a telegram over to Glory, to the sheriff there. Ask what has gone on in their town recently, if they know who that woman is. She works over at the eating house; you can find out her name from the proprietor."

"What if the good people of Glory don't know anything?"

"Well, we'll just have to wait around until Dodd comes back and we'll ask him."

"And if he doesn't?"

"Then I guess we wait for that marshal to arrive from Bridger. He can deal with it. I think I may have pushed Dodd as far as I can."

"Let's hope the marshal's good at what he does, 'cause that Dodd fella, he is not someone I would want to go up against."

"No." Silas rolled his tongue around his mouth and spat into the street. He wanted to voice his agreement, but thought it best to remain quiet. Since the killing of the family and the disappearance of Stoakes, nothing made sense. Dodd's arrival was no coincidence, Silas felt sure, and the woman ... Unconsciously, he eased his handgun from its holster and checked the load. A solution would come along, in its own good time, hopefully in the guise of the U.S. Marshal, telegrammed to come and investigate the killings. His only concern was how long he needed to wait and how much he needed to get involved.

Chapter Thirty-One

Arriving at Deep Water's cabin, White Dove took the horses to the little outhouse with its open front and roof of tarpaulin at the rear, whilst the men went inside, Simms to stock up the fire and Deep Water to bathe his wounded thigh.

Outside, as she unbuckled the saddles and laid them across a rail, White Dove stopped at the approach of the other woman. She smiled.

"My name is Melody," said the woman, stepping up close. "I never got the chance to thank you."

"I did not do so very much."

"You saved us from those awful savages and…" She stopped, noticing White Dove's dark stare. "I'm sorry, I didn't mean—"

"Many people believe all Natives are savages. Some are, most are not."

"I know, that's what I was trying to—"

"They must have wanted you bad to have come after you like that."

"One of them, he – he kidnapped me, I suppose you could say. Killed my best friend, trussed me up like a prize cow or something. I barely recall the name of the man who took me for his own. I tried to block everything out. Deep Water shot and killed him. He saved my life."

"Deep Water took you from their camp?"

"Yes. I'm not even sure why he did it, but …"

"He is Kiowa. He is brave, and is loyal to Simms. Perhaps he knows you?"

"No, I've never been this far west in my life before."

"He must have a reason. You must ask him."

"Yes, yes I will. And you – why are you with Simms?"

"I helped him when he was sick. In Fort Bridger. I have come to be close with him and …" She sucked in a breath, lowering her eyes for a moment. "I am Shoshone. The men who died, they were Shoshone too. I am sad for it."

"But you helped us. Without you—"

"No. Simms, he helped you. I did nothing, only watched."

"Even so …" She wringed her hands and moved closer. "I'm sorry for all of this. It was never my intention to cause so much pain and heartache. I was merely trying to get to Twin Buttes, to meet my father. Now, after what has happened, I doubt I'll ever get there."

"Deep Water, once he is well, will take you. Simms, he goes to Glory. He is sheriff there."

"And you will go with him."

"I do not know. The killing, it has made me sad. Simms is a good man, but I do not know." She went over to the horses and, with a handful of straw, brushed off the sweat and dirt from their naked backs. "I will come into the lodge when I am finished, then I will tend to Deep Water."

Melody pushed open the cabin door, the hinges screaming out her arrival. Deep Water looked at her over his shoulder, pausing for a moment in dabbing a blood soaked cloth into his wound. "Sit, rest. I will make us food."

"You need that leg seeing to."

"This? This is nothing. Once the flesh is soft enough, I shall pull the arrow out."

"Where's Simms?"

He arched a single eyebrow. "He washes himself, in the back. You have talked with the squaw?"

"Yes. She seems so sad. Apparently those Indians were her people."

"I know." He bent over and lowered the cloth into a basin filled with pink water. He grunted as he wrung the cloth out. She quickly came over to him, putting her hand over his. "I'll do it."

"I can do this my—"

"*I'll* do it." She wrested the cloth from his grip and twisted it in her hands, wringing out more water than he had managed. She eyed the wound, the arrow protruding from it. "I'm going to have cut that out."

"You can do such a thing?"

"My old pa used to do it sometimes. I watched. I learned."

"If you can do this …"

"If I don't it might fester. Then we'll need a doctor."

He grunted again and she took to dabbing the oozing yellow liquid seeping from the edges of the wound. "Why did you help me?"

At first, he did not speak, wincing a little as she applied pressure to soak the puckered flesh around the arrow. He took a breath. "I knew you were taken. I knew you had not been in the camp long. I have seen women such as you before. Most died."

"I'm grateful."

He snapped his head up and she recoiled at the burning in his glare, far greater than the newly-built fire raging close by. "Grateful? Do you think it pleased me to kill my friends? I traded with them and now, I can never go there again."

"I never asked for your help."

"No." He grew silent again, his eyes falling, the anger slipping away. "No, and I am sorry. I should not have—"

"We've all been through a lot," she said, soaking the cloth again, repeating the process, soaking the flesh. "I'm not sure I can go on much longer. First Nathan, now this … I wish to God I'd never left Kansas."

A shadow fell over her and she snapped her head up to see Simms standing there, shirtsleeves rolled up, braces hanging down by his side. "You need to rest. There'll be plenty of time to grieve over the coming days."

"Grieve? Sheriff, I have to thank you for saving us back there, but I'm not going to grieve. Anger, lots of that, regrets maybe."

"I overheard you talking about someone called Nathan? He was your husband?"

She spat out a sharp laugh. "Husband? Dear God no. He was a friend. A companion. There might have been a time when … But that Indian, he put paid to all of that. He killed Nathan then took me for his whore."

Simms screwed up his mouth and slowly pulled up the braces, one after the other. "We all handle things like this in our own way. Some of us swallow it deep, some of us go about doing chores and jobs and the like, anything to keep our minds off of it. Others, they cry. And some, hell, they just forget about it."

"Which one are you, Sheriff?"

"I've been around killing too long for it to get to me anymore. But you, you're not like that."

"Oh, but I am. I wanted to laugh when Deep Water killed that bastard. And I couldn't give a good damn for any of the men who died out on the prairie. None of them."

"Well, a lot of them did die, some more deserving than others."

She soaked the cloth again, this time taking more time in wringing it out. "I have to go to Twin Buttes. Keeping myself busy, perhaps."

"Well, my advice, if you'll take it, is to stay here until I get back."

"You're going to your town?"

"Glory? Yes, I am." He reached over and, taking the cloth from her hand, soaked it in the water then draped it, dripping wet, over the wound. He ignored Deep Water's sharp gasp. "I have to tidy up some business back there, then go across to Bovey and do much the same. If I don't get back there soon, people will think I've abandoned them – or got myself killed."

"When you get back, could you accompany me to Twin Buttes? My intention was to visit my father there before all this awfulness fell upon me."

"I shall. In the meantime, whilst you wait, I shall send a telegram to the sheriff there and enquire after your father."

"His name is Stoakes, Dan Stoakes. I'm obliged to you, Sheriff." She put her face in her hands and rubbed the skin with her palms. Bringing her hands down against her thighs with a slap she stood up. "I need to get out of these buckskins."

"I have no women's clothes," said Deep Water, looking startled.

"Then I'll borrow some of yours," she said and moved across to the entrance to the back room. "There are some washing things in there?"

"There's a jug of fresh water and a towel," said Simms, applying another squelching compress to the wound.

"Then that will have to do." She stepped over the threshold and closed the door behind her.

Simms and Deep Water exchanged a long look, but neither spoke. Words seemed redundant at that point.

Some time later, with the flesh soft and white, Simms held the Scout down whilst White Dove pushed in the knife and found the arrow point. Deep Water writhed. Melody had put the cloth into his mouth and he bit down on it hard, his back arching, eyes squeezed tight shut, tears sprouting from the corners. "Be quick," grunted Simms, pressing down on his friend's shoulders, "he's as strong as a goddamned longhorn."

"Take his ankles," said White Dove to Melody, who rushed to do her bidding.

With the Scout pinned, White Dove dug deeper.

Deep Water screamed, the sound muffled in the cloth, but terrible nevertheless.

And then it was free, the blood bubbling over his thigh, and White Dove held it in her hand like a trophy.

But Deep Water did not see. He had fainted.

Chapter Thirty-Two

"I want to take a look at the remains of the staging post."

They were trudging along a pass which cut a way through the soaring rocks on either side. Out here, with Bridger far behind, the temperature steadily rose, the air thick with insects.

"Jesus, it ain't even summer yet," said one of the two soldiers accompanying Marshal Dixon and Kieran Danks, stagecoach company owner. The soldier adjusted his position in his hard, unforgiving army issue saddle, tore off his neckerchief and wiped his dripping forehead.

"Did none of you hear me?" said Danks, pulling up his horse sharply. The animal's head reared up and it blew out a gust of breath from its flared nostrils.

"I heard you," said Dixon, bringing his own horse to a halt. "We have to clear this part of the trail first then, if we have the time, we can—"

"If we have the time? God damn you, Marshal, I told you I wanted to—"

"And I told you I needed to go to Twin Buttes first. Maybe you don't hear all that well, Kieran."

"We had a deal, damn you. We signed a contract."

Dixon flashed a look towards the two soldiers, who were sitting astride their own mounts, listening.

"Keep your voice down, Kieran. We made that deal when things were not so—"

"I'm sick of your prevaricating, Dixon. It was your idea to bring O'Shaughnessy in to guard my stage, and look what happened to that idea."

"No one could foresee Indians attacking the place. I reckon O'Shaughnessy was lucky to get out of there alive."

"Lucky? Well, to my mind, it sounds more than lucky. It sounds more like the whole damned thing was planned."

"Er, gentlemen," said one of the soldiers, "I think you should continue this discussion someplace else. We need to push on."

"Quite right," said Dixon.

"Shut the fuck up, private," spat Danks. "You're here to keep me safe, nothing more. Dixon, when I included that assurance clause, I had little idea I would need to claim on it quite so soon."

"Hell, Kieran, there is nothing suspicious about that."

"You think not? Accidental fire and destruction due to Indian attack? Convenient."

Dixon sighed. "Kieran. The only benefactors to that clause are you . . . and me. And any money we get will be put back into rebuilding the place."

"Unless I meet with an accident." Danks' eyes narrowed.

"What the hell are you talking about?"

"I think you know full well," said Danks; suddenly his hand appeared, filled with the revolver from the holster at his hip. "I'm good with this, make no mistake."

One of the soldiers cried out in alarm; the young lieutenant accompanying them all threw up his hand, "Now hang on there, Mr Danks, you have no cause to—"

Danks turned in his saddle and shot the young lieutenant in the chest, the bullet hurling him off his saddle, sending him crashing to the ground. Crying out for a second time, the other soldier turned his maddened horse away and spurred it into a gallop.

"Holy shit," said Dixon between clamped teeth. "You just shot Lieutenant Miers."

Danks turned his gun on Dixon. "Yes, and you'll be next if you don't tell me what is going on."

"Going on? With what?"

"You think I don't know what you're doing, Dixon? You think I don't know you mean to kill me out here and claim all that money for yourself?"

With his hands raised, Dixon's breath trickled out, his voice fractious, trembling, "Kieran, you got all this wrong."

"I don't think so."

"Jesus, you've just shot dead an officer of the United States Army. What in the hell are you thinking of?"

"I'm thinking of you taking me to that staging post, so I can get a good look at it, then I'm thinking of making the claim."

"You can't. That soldier, he'll get back to Bridger and tell them all what happened here. You're out of your mind if you think you can get away with it."

"It'll be my word against his. Besides, I have no intention of going back to Bridger. I'm relocating."

"You're *what*? Where to?"

"I'm not going to tell you that, you bastard. Now throw me that revolver of yours, then lead on towards the staging post. Once my suspicions are verified, that you and O'Shaughnessy were in cahoots together, I'll decide what happens next."

"The hell you will. You've got this way off beam, Kieran."

Danks eased back the hammer of his Colt. "Give me your gun."

Dixon's hand moved to his holster.

"Nice and easy, Dixon, or I'll shoot you right here."

"You'll never make it on your own, Kieran."

"You let me worry about that. Give me your gun."

Taking his time, Dixon picked out his gun by his thumb and forefinger and threw it across to Danks, who made no move to catch it, watching it land in the dirt. He chuckled.

"This territory is a dangerous place," said Dixon, "if we get lost …" He nodded to his jacket. "I have a map."

"A map? All right, give it me – and this time, don't throw it; hand it over, nice and slow."

Without a word, Dixon reached inside his coat and brought out the folded map. Danks held out his hand. In a blur, Dixon hurled the map through the air before plunging back into his jacket to bring out a single-shot, muzzle loading pocket pistol, which he discharged without a pause.

The ball struck Danks in the lower jaw, blowing him backwards but not with the same effect as Danks' own gunshot some moments earlier. He clung on to his reins whilst his horse reared up, screaming with terror. He flailed about, lost his grip and fell.

Dixon, not waiting to admire his handiwork, jumped down and swept up his fallen revolver. Even before Danks fell, he was bringing the gun to bear and shot the stagecoach owner three times in the body.

The sound of the shots reverberated around the close confines of the looming rocks. The only other sound was that of the horses' hooves pounding away in every direction as they bolted.

Dixon stood, his smoking gun in his trembling hand, and he realised he was totally alone. The horses were gone.

Chapter Thirty-Three

They rode at a steady pace, making good time. The day, cold and sharp, was in their favour and the trail ran like an arrow across the prairie, the sunlight reflecting from its hard-packed surface. Simms, straight in the saddle, senses alert, remained silent whilst White Dove cantered by his side, her eyes roaming the distant horizon. Both were aware of the dangers lurking all around them. Raiding parties were becoming more frequent as of late; Deep Water warned them to be forever watchful. Approaching Glory, the cluster of buildings appearing grey and gloomy, both sighed with relief. On reaching Main Street, they exchanged a smile.

People bustled through the narrow street, some stopping to tilt their hats as Simms reined in his horse, whilst others frowned with barely disguised hostility towards White Dove, who met their stares with a defiance.

"They probably think you're part of a Ute war party," sniggered Simms and stepped onto the boardwalk. He tried the handle of the office door and it creaked open.

It appeared much as he'd left it. Even the empty bottle stood unmoved on his desk. He ran a finger down it, thoughts slipping back to the day Martinson found him slumped in the corner.

"It is cold," said White Dove, coming into the room, breath steaming in the air. She put down their saddle bags and went over to the small belly-stove in the corner, working at clearing away the clinker in the grate with a blackened fork she picked up from the corner.

Simms rifled through an assortment of papers lying on the desk. Most were warrants, with several communications from Laramie and a telegram from Illinois. Short and to the point, his office wanted a report of his actions concerning Tabatha and the charges made against her and her mother. Closing his eyes, images dancing in front of him, Simms swallowed down the bile as he recalled how his old friend Martinson had been brutalised, humiliated and terrorised. One day the reckoning would come between him and Tabatha.

"*Simms,* where in the name of merry hell have you been?"

Simms looked up to see Richard Toft, mayor-designate of Glory, filling the doorway. A large man, he wore an ill-fitting black frock coat and matching Stetson. Jutting his chin out, his cheeks glowing fiery red, Toft's gaze settled on White Dove, on her knees before the wood-stove. "Well, well. Got yourself some company, so it seems."

Simms sighed, put the telegram from the Pinkerton Agency aside and sat down behind his desk. "I was delayed."

"You can say that again." Toft moved inside and closed the door behind him. "This is not what we agreed to, Simms – your time was to be shared between Bovey and us. Why in the hell did you high-tail it out to Bridger?"

"I got sidetracked. It happens."

"Well, it shouldn't, damn you. Your duty is here, as sheriff of this town. We discussed all this."

"If you need to reconsider our agreement, Richard, then that is your prerogative."

"Elections are coming up soon enough, Simms – but hell, I *want* you in this post. We need to get this town back on its feet after what happened with that Shelby character. The way he waltzed in here, shot the place up. What he did. People will be forever grateful to you, Simms. We don't want anything like that to happen again."

"Well, then you need to give me some space, Richard. I have to go over to Bovey and—"

"But you've only just got here and now you're going away again?"

"I'm taking White Dove over to Martinson's. From there he'll help her settle into my ranch. I'll be away two days. Perhaps less."

Simms could see the inner conflict etched into every worry line on Toft's face.

"I will not keep him long," said White Dove, stepping away from the fire, now alight. She closed the grill door and brushed off her hands on her breeches.

Opening his mouth, Toft stopped, looked into her eyes and smiled. The tension left his shoulders. "Well, little lady, what am I supposed to say to that?"

She shrugged, cheeks reddening slightly. "When he returns, he is all yours."

And they all laughed as the atmosphere grew lighter. "Two days," said Toft.

Simms nodded and waited until the mayor-to-be went out.

"Is that your plan? To let me settle into your ranch?"

"Is it not what you want?"

"You know what I want, but I wonder if you coming here alone again is not such a good idea."

"You worry too much," he said as he stood up and came around the desk to hold her in his arms.

"No," she said softly, voice muffled in his chest. "I feel something. Something not good. You are going to go to Twin Buttes, aren't you, with Melody?"

"To help her find her father, yes. It's what I promised."

"It is that which causes me fear, Simms. I think you will find that other woman there, the woman you often speak of."

"Tabatha? Well, I'm not sure where she is, but if she is at Twin Buttes, then I suppose fate will bring us together. She's a murderess, White Dove, with a wicked streak a mile wide running down her back. "

"And it is that which frightens me. I will come with you."

"I want you in the ranch, to keep it warm, so that when I return we can—"

"It will never be warm if you are dead in the dirt, Simms."

He pulled in a breath and looked down into her troubled eyes. "What makes you say that?"

"She wants you dead. I think she is waiting for you, out there in the prairie. I think she has done those terrible things in this Twin Buttes town, to lure you into her trap."

"You're wrong."

"How can you be sure?"

He went to speak, but the realisation that White Dove's fears may well be grounded caused him to stop and reconsider. He expelled air hard through his nostrils. "Listen, we'll go down to Martinson, check all is well in Bovey, then we'll both go over to Twin Buttes. What do you say to that?"

"I say that is the best plan you have had all day."

She laughed and he drew her closer, kissing her on the mouth, pushing away the negative thoughts threatening to overtake him.

With the taste and feel of her soft mouth, he almost succeeded.

But not quite.

Chapter Thirty-Four

Long before he collapsed, Dixon shredded his jacket and gunbelt and tramped as if in a daze across the harsh, barren plain.
No longer aware of his surroundings, his mind a confusion of
shapes, sounds, colours and images, the one overpowering sen-
sation his burning throat, gradually growing drier with each
passing step. Above him, the sun beat down, not as strong as in
summer but still unbearable. Listless, the strength drained from
his muscles, he stumbled and fell, gasping as his knees struck the
hard earth. From somewhere, he dragged up the last remnants
of his strength and zigzagged towards an outcrop of rock, the
hope of some shade and respite acting like a magnet. Looking
out through blurred eyes, he staggered forward, hands thrust
out like a blind man, groping in the darkness of his despair.

Collapsing to the ground, he rolled over, back against the cool
rock, a pool of shade his world. His one comfort. Eyelids heavy,
he surrendered to his exhaustion. With no idea how long he had
trudged across the endless plain, the horses gone, no chance of
water, he knew his life would end out here. Alone, forgotten,
food for the buzzards which already flew overhead, waiting for
the moment to swoop and feast on his flesh. Groaning, he allowed himself to slide onto his side and close his eyes to sleep.

It may have been a minute, perhaps ten hours, he did not
know, but when the shadow fell over him he woke with a start,

instinctively going for the gun no longer at his hip. A face loomed over him, the sun like a halo around it. An angel? Was he already in heaven? A man like him? No, this could not be heaven. Maybe this was a demon from the bowels of hell? He whimpered, not having the strength to speak or care.

A cool hand pressed itself on his forehead, followed by the ecstasy of water. A few drops, dabbed across his lips, just enough to revitalise, caused him to go into a gut-wrenching spasm of coughing. A strong arm held him, lifting him. A little more water, hitting the back of his throat like burning coals. He retched and a voice, distant, ephemeral, floated to him like liquid honey. "Be still, my friend."

The world became one of flashing lights, of barely discernible movements and images around the periphery of his vision. Strong hands lifting him, a wet cloth dragged over his face. The sight of passing ground. Confused, unable to disentangle any meaning, he lapsed once more into the comforting embrace of sleep.

When next he woke, his eyes settled upon a wooden ceiling. Bare, roughly hewn tree trunks, pitch between each, and a candle burning somewhere, giving off a faint, flickering glow. Voices, more than one. More water, his mouth eagerly lapping up the wondrous liquid; a hand, cool, resting upon him. Another face. So beautiful. Eyes of blue, a mouth soft, lips full, skin smooth, golden. A true angel.

Heavenly.

Yes.

No more fear now. He was home.

"You must try and eat something."

The voice spurred him to open his eyes again, take in his surroundings and prop himself up on his elbow. He saw he was in a cabin. A small, cramped place, a fire burning in the corner, a pot bubbling amongst the crackling, sizzling wood. Another door, set in the far wall, stood closed. A small window offered meagre light. From the ceiling hung various utensils, hunks of smoked meat, an ancient bath tub.

"It's bean broth," said the angel, sitting beside him, long hair hanging in two plaits framing a face of startling loveliness. Her eyes shone with such kindness, Dixon wanted to cry out and give thanks for all she had done.

The smell of the food wafted into his nostrils and his stomach lurched with hunger. She helped him, putting one arm around his neck whilst in her other hand she brought up a wooden spoon filled with broth. He took a small mouthful, closing his eyes in rapture as the liquid slipped down his throat.

As she fed him, her voice came, floating on the air. "Deep Water found you out on the prairie. He came across your horses and followed their tracks back to you."

He looked at her as she tipped another spoonful of food into his mouth.

"He found two bodies. Shot dead." She took away the bowl, now finished, and dabbed at his mouth with a cloth. "You were ambushed?"

Dixon swallowed. Whoever this woman was, she was responsible for saving his life. Her and the one she called Deep Water, wherever he was. There was no point in lying, not anymore. He cleared his throat, voice rough, brittle. "No. The man I was with, he tried to kill me."

Her expression did not alter. "Why would he do that?"

"We were partners. He double-crossed me, killed the other, a lieutenant in the army. I managed to shoot him but the horses bolted, with all of my provisions."

"Deep Water found you close to death. No gun, no water."

"And I'm so grateful, I truly am."

Her eyes, boring into him, the grand inquisitor. "He found your things." She turned, allowing Dixon to catch a view across the room to a hard-backed chair. Draped over the back was his coat, gunbelt and hat. "No gun. How did you shoot this other man?"

He shuffled uneasily on the bed. It was a narrow piece of furniture, the mattress threadbare, stuffed with straw or some such material, hard and uncomfortable. Her words too made him uneasy, as if she doubted him, perhaps believing him to be the aggressor. If he could not convince her, the man who saved him, the one she called Deep Water, would he turn aggressive, even dangerous? "He had the drop on me but I had a small pistol, concealed in my coat. I shot him with it."

This time, when she turned her face towards him, the features were changed, the eyes soft, the mouth upturned into a small smile. "There is a badge on your coat. A Marshal's badge."

"That is what I am. A U.S. Marshal. I got a telegram from Twin Buttes whilst stationed at Fort Bridger. There was some trouble there and—"

"Wait," she said, stepping closer, her face once again turning serious. "Did you say Twin Buttes?"

"Yes. It's a small town not so far from—"

"I know where it is. My father, he sent me a—"

The main door opened, sending a blast of chill air into the confines of the cabin. Deep Water stood there, carbine in one hand, jack-rabbit in the other. He seemed to be assessing the situation in front of him and, by the look on his face, appeared none too pleased.

The girl went to him without a word and hugged him. She took the rabbit and moved across to the small table nestling under the single window and took to skinning the animal with a sharp knife. Dixon watched her before turning his gaze on the Indian who remained motionless, tall and grim. "I'm glad you're here," he said, voicing the first thoughts that came into his head. "I wanted to thank you, for saving my life."

The Indian grunted and closed the door behind him. He propped the carbine in the corner and pulled off his thick overcoat. Underneath this he wore a simple cloth shirt, cut off at the shoulders, revealing arms swollen with muscle, flesh gleaming. Dodd, feeling the strain of sitting up for too long, collapsed onto his back and gave a shuddering sigh. "I'm in your debt."

Another grunt and the Indian went to the other door set within the wall and disappeared inside. Dixon craned his neck, noticing the Indian walked with a limp.

The girl looked over her shoulder. "Don't mind him – he never says very much."

"I get the feeling he doesn't want me here. How long has it been since he found me?"

"Two days."

"Jeez … I'm sorry."

Grunting, she went back to her work, pulled away the skin of the rabbit before slicing up the flesh and dropping hunks into a waiting metal pot. "I didn't know you were going to Twin Buttes. I plan to go there myself, as soon as Simms gets back."

Her words sounded like his death knell and Dixon, mouth parting slightly, struggled to control his breathing. "Simms?"

"A friend. He saved *my* life, in a way. Deep Water and he are very close. We were set upon by some desperadoes, then a war-party of Shoshone warriors came. It was all very terrible." She turned around, leaning back against the table, using an old piece of rag to wipe hands smeared with rabbit's blood. She frowned. "What's the matter? You look frightened."

"No, no, I'm … I'm fine." He forced a chuckle. "Just tired, I guess."

"Then rest. Later we will have supper and you can sleep."

"Tomorrow. Tomorrow I will leave for Twin Buttes."

"Tomorrow? I'm not sure if you will be well enough to travel."

"I'll be fine – and you, you can come with me."

Tilting her head, frown growing deeper, she considered him for a long time. "It would be best if we waited for Simms. He knows the territory better than most. He will protect us."

"He will?"

"Yes. I know it. Deep Water says he is the finest man alive. A man most proficient in firearms, he says."

Failing to disguise a deep swallow, Dixon merely grinned before rolling over onto his side. His eyes closed and his heartbeat raced. Of all things, to be trapped here with Simms falling over him like some sort of avenging angel, it would have been better to have died out on the prairie.

"You rest," came her voice. "Then we will decide what to do."

But Dixon had already decided. There really was no other choice.

To kill Simms out on the prairie ... with the Indian's carbine.

Chapter Thirty-Five

Martinson came running out of the merchant store with his arms spread wide, as wide as the grin on his face. Jumping down from his horse, Simms embraced him, beaming. "I thought I'd never see you again," said Martinson, breathless.

"Never think that, my friend."

Slapping him on the back, Martinson pointed across to where White Dove sat astride her horse. "Who's this?"

"This is White Dove," said Simms. "She's another friend. Well …" He grew awkward, heat rising to his cheeks. "If you get my meaning."

Nodding, Martinson went across to White Dove and held out his hand. "Good to know you, White Dove."

She smiled and took his hand. "I have heard much about you."

"Oh?" He turned a quizzical look towards Simms. "Nothing bad, I hope."

"No, all good."

"Well hell's bells," he cried, "go and put the horses in the stable, then come and get some food inside you. You'll be going to Bovey, to check on things no doubt."

As White Dove steered the two horses over to the outhouse which served as a stable, Martinson and Simms strolled over to the merchant's store and went inside.

The store served as both a shop and an eating place, the only such establishment before the vast expanse of the Colorado plain stretched forever onward towards the horizon. Once this place had teemed with prospectors, whores and chancers as the Gold Rush attracted every form of human life imaginable. But that was years before. Now, virtually deserted, Martinson clung on to a life that was hard and tedious, with little financial reward.

He stepped behind the counter and poured Simms a beer, half of the glass filled with froth. The Pinkerton blew off the top and drank fitfully, smacking his lips with relish. Martinson watched and smiled. "Good trip?"

"Nope."

Martinson leaned his palms on top of the counter. "I figured as much when you didn't get back. What happened?"

"Oh, not much. I fell ill with some sort of pneumonia, then was beaten half to death for a crime I didn't commit. Broke free, thanks to White Dove, helped out Deep Water caught between a bunch of killers and a band of Indians, then moved on to Glory to receive a lecture from that bastard Richard Toft." He shrugged, smiling at Martinson's bemused expression. "Like I said, not much."

"Holy Mother," breathed the Swede, taking away Simms' glass and refilling it. Before Simms could take it, Martinson downed it for himself.

"I need you to do me a favour."

"Anything," said Martinson, refilling the glass again, but this time pushing it across to Simms.

"I'm taking White Dove to the ranch. I need you to look in on her now and then. I'm making my way over to Twin Buttes, sort out one or two things there. I'll call in on Bovey on the way." He shook his head, feeling awkward. "I said she could come with me, but the more I think of it, the more I'm certain I'm heading into trouble. She has an inkling Tabatha will be at Twin Buttes. She could be right."

Martinson paled. "Tabatha? Holy Mother of God. She'll kill you, Simms."

"She'll try, bless her heart." He drank more beer.

Martinson chewed at his lower lip and nodded towards Simms' waist. "Where are your guns?"

"Took. By the bastards who arrested me. Lost my Dragoon, my Navy and that little pistol Pinkerton gave me. I've got my old Patersons back in the ranch, so I'll load up with them. They'll do the job, I guess."

"You expecting trouble over at Twin Buttes?"

"More than trouble. If I do find Tabatha over there…" The blood drained from Martinson's face and Simms quickly reached across and squeezed his friend's forearm. "Don't."

"That bitch would have sliced off my manhood if you hadn't—"

Simms grunted. "Don't."

The door opened and White Dove came in, rubbing herself with her hands, "It has gone cold. The night draws in."

"I'll make coffee," said Martinson, embarrassed, his eyes wet, mouth trembling.

He disappeared into the back room and White Dove stepped up to Simms. "He is upset?"

"Memories is all."

"Bad ones?"

"Very bad."

They reached the ranch house with the sun well below the horizon, the evening sky tinged with pink and purple. Inside, the cold hit them like blows and White Dove set upon preparing the stove, just as she had done back in Glory. Simms smiled. "I could get used to this."

"I hope so," she said with a smile.

He found the old battered case in the back room, pushed under his bed. Inside was his army uniform from his Mexican War days, and the twin Colt Patersons that had served him so well in that conflict. He checked them and sighed. Almost ten long years since they were last fired. They'd need plenty of cleaning and priming, but they would serve him well, as they had done all that time ago. He eased back the hammer and the trigger snapped into place underneath. Later model, 1836, with loading lever and point thirty-six calibre. Squinting down the barrel he eased off a shot and everything worked just as crisply as when he first used them. Smiling, he took both guns with him into the main room and prepared to disassemble and make them ready for live firing once more.

White Dove stood and watched.

After a few moments, he caught her stare. "I won't be long."

"You are planning on fighting again."

"It's what I do."

"Yes. But who is it this time?"

"The woman who almost murdered Martinson – who also tried to murder me. But more than that. Something isn't right with what's going on over at Twin Buttes. I mean to go to Bovey, send a telegram, find out why the town sent for a marshal."

"But that has nothing to do with you."

"It might have everything to do with me. There was a marshal at Bridger, if you remember."

"Yes. I remember him well. I fear him. I fear for you if you go there, to this place and find him there. That is what you believe, yes?"

He nodded and went back to cleaning out the chambers in the cylinders.

"I do not like it. What if he has men with him? What if he shoots you and kills you? What do I do then?"

"It won't happen."

"At least you said I could come with you."

"I've changed my mind."

"Changed … ? You cannot! You said."

"I know what I said, but I've been thinking. It's going to be too dangerous. I can't go into a fight worrying about you – I'd lose my edge. Besides, it may all be nothing."

"You cannot be sure. I do not want you to go. I want you to stay here, with me."

Her eyes locked on his and he saw the tears welling up. Putting down the gun, he stood up and went to her. Holding her, he breathed her in, closed his eyes and wished he was any-one else but who he was. "I'm a lawman," he said quietly, "A Pinkerton and a sheriff. There are some things that just need doing, is all."

"And there are some things which you can leave alone. I have a bad feeling."

"You said all that before. It's nothing but—"

"No. It is a sign. A prophesy. You cannot go on your own. I must come with you."

"You can't. I want you to stay here. I've already told Martin-son to—"

"I come with you, Simms. You are my man and I will not let you go alone."

And when he looked into her eyes he saw there was no argu-ing with her. So he sighed, smiled and held her close. Perhaps, if he held her long enough, all the bad feelings would drift away.

Perhaps.

Chapter Thirty-Six

Striding across the main street first thing the following morning, Richard Toft stifled a yawn. He needed to make an early start, visit the local news press and arrange for some posters to be distributed around town. Rubbing his chin, having been in too much of a rush to shave, he hoped he might get everything finished before lunch.

But then he saw the horses tied up outside the saloon and pulled up sharp. He didn't like the look of the carbines in their scabbards. He liked even less the surly-looking youth chewing on a stalk of grass, leaning against the sun-canopy post, most especially the tied down guns.

"Shit," he muttered.

The youth considered Toft for a moment, straightened himself and twisted his scrawny neck towards the double bat-wing doors, yelling, "You better come see this."

Toft, the fear gripping him, wanted to turn in retreat, but a weird feeling embraced him, an inability to move his legs. So he stood, rooted and trembling, knowing none of this was any good.

A man came out from the saloon, tall and slim. He wore a silver-threaded waistcoat and a tall black hat. His white shirt appeared pristine and he chewed on a sliver of bacon. Raising a single eyebrow, he smiled. "Ah, a town dignitary by the looks of him."

Toft watched the man's approach, his eyes falling on the revolver at his hip. These were not businessmen or gold miners. Nor were they lawmen. Gunhands, bounty hunters. Killers.

Beyond the immaculately attired stranger, three more appeared on the boardwalk, one of them a woman, strikingly pretty. Even she wore a gun. Toft squeaked, "I ..."

The man closest held up his hand. "Good morning to you. My name is Dodd. My associates and I are on some personal business and it looks to me like you could be of some assistance."

"I don't really think I—"

"We tried asking the barkeep, but he was less than forthcoming. You, on the other hand, will provide me with what I want to know." He smiled and chewed down the last piece of bacon. "Or I'll blow a hole in your head."

Toft's bowel loosened at that point. His legs gave way and he collapsed to his knees, whimpering. The stranger, screwing up his face, took an involuntary step backwards. "Oh my, that is quite disgusting."

A voice shouted. A distant voice, from the far end of the street. Through his misery, Toft managed to pick out the shape of Tom Shanks, one of the deputies whom Toft wanted to help look after things until Simms returned. Toft opened his mouth, brought up a warning hand – *stay back, for god's sake stay—*

A single shot rang out, breaking the quiet of the morning, and Toft looked in disbelief as the bullet struck Shanks in the chest, hurling him to the ground where he lay, arms and legs spread-eagled, quite dead.

"Oh Jesus."

"Nice shot," breathed the stranger, blowing down the barrel of his still smoking revolver. He got down on his haunches, peering into Toft's face. "Wasn't sure if I'd hit him from this range, but Mr Samuel Colt never fails to amaze me with his precision engineering. I used to carry a Star, but much prefer this little beauty." He tipped back his hat with the barrel of his Colt Navy. "I want to know where Simms is."

Frowning, Toft shook his head, confused, lost in a world of fear and anguish. Simms? Why would this monster want Simms?

The man's eyes narrowed. "I ain't gonna ask you twice."

"Bovey," said Toft quickly, hands coming up, desperate now. "Bovey. He headed out there the other day, then he's going to Twin Buttes."

The man's eyes closed for a moment. "Is that the truth?"

"Yes, yes it is. Jesus God, why would I lie to you after ... After *that*?"

Seeing the sense in this argument, Dodd stood up and stretched out his back. As he dropped his revolver into its holster, the girl came up alongside him. "Did he tell you?"

"Simms has gone to Bovey, then back to Twin Buttes."

"He's lying."

"No, I don't think so. Poor fella shit himself. He's too afraid to lie, ain't you?"

Toft nodded frantically.

"Then we ride on down to Bovey."

Dodd took a deep breath. "Might be best. Finish up in the saloon, then get the boys together. This is turning into a mighty big waste of time, Tabby."

"Not if we find Simms it ain't. I want that bastard strung up before nightfall."

"So you've said." Dodd looked down at Toft. "But I have an idea. We send a telegram, maybe two. Get him to come to us. That way we can be ready, meet him head on."

"Sounds good."

Dodd again looked at Toft. "If you've lied to me, I'll cut off your balls before I put a bullet in your brain. You know that, don't you?"

Toft nodded.

"Oh fuck this," spat Tabatha and whipped out her own firearm.

Toft saw it, but only sensed a bright flash of light.

Then nothing at all.

Chapter Thirty-Seven

The street ached. Both sensed it. Dixon, on the lead horse, pulled his mount to a halt and leaned over to his left, peering down at the dirt.

"What is it?"

He barely turned to acknowledge her, grunting, "Blood."

Melody drew up alongside him, her eyes roaming over the deathly quiet buildings. Not yet noon; the town should have been alive with people, but the atmosphere of dread hung over everything. A funeral shroud, ominous and heavy. "I don't like this place."

"Me neither," said Dixon, straightening his back. He gestured towards the sheriff's office. "We might get an answer there."

"And if we don't?"

"Then I guess we try the assayer's office. Someone must know what's been going on."

"I just want to find my father."

"I know. And so we shall."

Kicking his horse, he crossed over to the sheriff's and slipped down from his saddle. Melody sat quietly, not making any movement to follow him. He raised a quizzical eyebrow. She shrugged. "You go ahead, I'll wait."

Grunting, he stepped up onto the boardwalk and tried the door. To his surprise, it creaked open and he stepped inside.

The sheriff was sweeping the small, iron barred jail room when Dixon came in. He stopped and studied Dixon with eyes burning with a latent fury.

"Are you looking for Simms?"

Dixon had to force himself not to squawk at the sound of the Pinkerton's name.

"Or Dodd? Neither of them are here."

"Actually," said Dixon, pulling off his hat and wiping the inside rim with his neckerchief, "It's Dan Stoakes I'm after."

"Really? And what would you be wanting with him?"

"I have his daughter outside."

The sheriff cocked his head and threw the broom into the corner, "Well I'll be damned. Bring her in, why don't you."

"I think she's kinda fearful of what she might hear regarding her pa. Best if you tell me where I can find the old man."

Stepping into the office, the sheriff brought the cell door closed with a clang and plodded over to his desk. With a loud sigh he flopped down into his chair. "Wish I could help you. The little lady too, but I can't."

"And why's that?"

"Because I don't know where he is."

"So I heard."

"So you heard? What in the hell is that supposed to me—"

He drew back his jacket to reveal the badge pinned to his waistcoat. "My name is Dixon. *Marshal* Dixon, and I'm here in answer to the telegram you sent to Fort Bridger."

Dixon spent a long time leaning on his knuckles, studying Quincy's discarded coat draped across the desk before him. "And this Dodd, you think he put those two sonsofbitches in the ground?"

"Seems a mite strange to me that no sooner does he arrive, that the silver mine is abandoned and those two boys are dead."

"And old Dan?"

"No sign of him. I reckon Quincy and Charlie did for him. They made a counter claim and it was never disputed."

"Melody is his daughter."

"So you said."

"She's gonna want to find his body. Any thoughts on where it might be?"

"Nope. We scoured the surrounding area, but didn't find a trace. I'm guessing they burned the body."

Dixon pressed his lips together. "And this Dodd, he took over the claim?"

"He said he knew old Dan, although in what regard I have no idea. Maybe Dan's daughter knows."

Nodding, Dixon straightened himself up. "She'll be taking over the mine. It's hers by birthright."

"You'll have to clear that with the assayer. Dodd has his claim."

"Dodd's ain't worth shit, not now that Melody is here."

"She can prove she is Dan's daughter?"

"She has all the necessary documentation."

"Dodd ain't gonna like it. He'll face you, Marshal. I've known a lot of rattlers in my time, but I ain't ever known a man like him; he carries the scent of death with him."

"You've witnessed what he is capable of."

"I *know* what he is capable of. He's ridden down to Glory to face that Simms character. I reckon when he comes back, Dodd will seek some form of recompense over the mine."

"I doubt he'll be coming back, Sheriff."

"Simms can't be that good."

For an answer, Dixon merely smiled and pushed past Silas, pausing only to tap him on the arm. "I'm taking Melody to the mine, then I'll finalise the legalities. Other than that, I think my business is done here."

Outside, the sun high in the sky, Dixon stretched out his arms and yawned. Too many days in the saddle brought tension to his joints, many of which cracked as he flexed himself.

Melody sat hunched over the pommel of her saddle, her breathing heavy, and Dixon touched the hem of her jacket with his fingertips. She gave a little moan and turned her head to face him.

Her skin appeared waxen, grey, the eyes red-rimmed, the lips blue, drained of blood.

He gasped and took a tiny step backwards. "Melody … Good God Almighty, are you all right?"

A fleeting smile and then she was crumpling over the side of her horse. He caught her in his arms and laid her slowly to the ground, cradling her, brushing away the strands of lank hair sticking to her wet forehead.

"What's happened to her?"

It was Silas, standing in his office doorway, face tense with concern.

"I don't know," said Dixon, never taking his eyes from her. "Some sort of fever. She must have been feeling sick for some time, but didn't say a word."

"You should get her into bed, Marshal. Shall I call the Doc?"

"I'll take her to the mine. She'll be fine."

"If she has fever, you need to be care—"

"I said I'm taking her to the mine, Goddamn it. As soon as she's settled, I'll call in at the assayer's office."

Silas remained still as Dixon lifted Melody into the saddle and hauled himself up behind her. Without a word, Silas went over to Dixon's horse and handed its reigns over to the Marshal, who then turned away and left the town at an easy gait.

He applied a cloth soaked in warm water to her brow. She lay on the poor excuse of a mattress in the broken down old shack Stoakes used for his dwelling. Her eyes fluttered open.

"I'm sorry," she managed to say, her voice little more than a croak.

"Don't you worry none," he said.

"My father … If you find him …"

"It's all taken care of, Melody. When you're well, we'll make a fortune from this place. I've seen the lode with my own eyes. We'll be rich."

A flickering of a smile. "I feel so …"

"I know," he said, taking the cloth from her brow and pressing it firmly against her nose and mouth, pinning her arms with his knees. Her struggle proved feeble and short, her body weak from the sickness. Being such a slight thing, he would have had little difficulty overcoming her even if she were at full fitness.

It took little more than a minute for her life to fade away.

He rocked back on his heels and studied her lifeless form. In another lifetime, in different circumstances, perhaps he could have forged a life with a girl such as her. But the opportunity for riches proved too much; his greed and avarice won through right to the end.

All he needed to do now was secure the claim, then face either Dodd or Simms. Neither seemed a good prospect, but at least he knew something of Simms and his capabilities. He shrugged them off, for his own abilities were substantial and he harboured few doubts over who would prevail.

With that thought, he grinned to himself and prepared a beef stew supper whilst Melody's body lay rigid and ghastly in the murky confines of the shack.

Chapter Thirty-Eight

The telegraph operator came running up in a flap, eyes wide with alarm, mouth blubbering. Simms, still in the process of dismounting outside his office, motioned for White Dove to stay saddled. He dropped down.

"Mr Simms, I sure am glad you're here."

Simms frowned and took the proferred message.

"It's from Glory. Terrible thing. This is the second one. Four hours ago."

Simms read the simple message. Single words, so stark, so telling. '*Gunmen in Glory, stop. Toft killed, stop. Help needed, stop.*'

"The second one?" said Simms.

"First one just rattled out, 'Two killed. Send for Simms.'"

"It sounds like a trap," said White Dove.

Simms sucked in his bottom lip. "I reckon so."

"So what will you do?" asked the operator.

Simms sighed. "Just exactly what they want me to." He winked, screwed up the message and hurled it away.

"Are you sure, Mr Simms, because if all of this is true, then—"

"I'm sure. Toft may be dead, he may not. I'll know once I get there. In the meantime, I want you to run off a cable to Bridger. I want you to ask them what they know of the trouble in Twin Buttes and how the U.S. Marshal has reacted. You do that as soon as you can."

Without a word, the operator scurried off. Simms turned to White Dove. "Looks like the fates have conspired once again."

"They will ambush you as you ride into town."

"I know. Which is why we circumnavigate and come at them from behind."

"Circum-*what*?"

"Oh, just an old Indian trick." He grinned and went through the door of his office, leaving White Dove to mutter something in Shoshone behind him.

Simms took his time in his office, filling out various reports ready to send over to Chicago. He checked his revolvers and the Halls carbine, greasing up the cylinders of the Patersons, cleaning out the breech of the carbine. He settled down to placing the prepared paper cartridges inside a small leather pouch. The Halls, although a single-shot rifle, was easy to load, holding one paper cartridge in the breech. During the Mexican War, such a gun had saved his life more than once. For a moment he studied it, his thoughts returning to that conflict, how his young life changed, all innocence gone. He recalled the day after the powers-that-be signed the treaty ending the war, how his commanding officer gathered them at their camp inside the once disputed territory of New Mexico, telling them how a new compromise would settle the disputes within the area forever. "This would be a good time to find yourselves some land, to settle," said their commander, Randall, sitting astride his big white stallion, a fine, straight man, bold as they come.

Simms recalled the heat of that day, the expressions on the faces of the men, their uncertainty. Many longed to return home; perhaps more experienced trepidation for what awaited them. For his own part, Simms decided to take his horse and wander across to Santa Fe, no particular plans forming in his mind.

And then came news that one of the senators brokering The Compromise was from Illinois, and he spoke of a new enforcement agency being planned over in Chicago. With nothing to lose, Simms travelled east and put in his application. Allan Pinkerton himself countersigned the application. Detective Simms.

Chuckling to himself, Simms reached across his desk and sifted through the letters piled up before him. Nothing urgent, but the one from the Chicago office intrigued him. He read it through before folding it neatly and dropping it in his shirt pocket.

From the far side of the room, White Dove came over with a plate of beans and corn tortillas, which she had prepared in the rear yard over a scratch built oven. Simms eyed them, impressed. "They look good."

"When do we go?"

He paused in the act of taking a bite. "Listen, I'm still not convinced you should—"

"We no longer speak of that," she said, her eyes blazing with renewed anger. "Nothing you can say will stop me from being by your side. So stop."

Holding up his hand in surrender, Simms took a bite and munched down the food, juice drizzling down his chin. She leaned over and dabbed at his chin with her neckerchief. He smiled as she moved closer and kissed him. She licked her lips. "That tastes good."

The tortilla dropped from his fingers and in a rush he came around the table, seizing her, pulling away her dress, her hands delving into his trousers. They fell to the floor, their need all-consuming.

Afterwards they lay spent on their backs, breathing hard, gazing at the ceiling.

"I wonder what Mr. Pinkerton would say if he knew what went on in his only office out west?"

"He might be excited."

He chuckled and turned to face her. "I doubt it. The man is too straight-laced for that."

"Do you care what he thinks?"

"No. I don't care what anybody thinks."

"About us?"

Simms nodded.

"There are many who would object to a respectable lawman having a squaw for a lover."

"I ain't that respectable. Besides, I don't think of you as a squaw – I think of you as the woman I love. And to hell with anyone else and their narrow-minded ways."

Her eyes grew wide and, for a moment, she appeared to struggle to find her breath. When he reached out to stroke her braided hair, she gripped his hand. "You mean that?"

"What? That I love you? Of course I do."

She pressed herself close and he held her. At one point he felt tiny sobs shuddering from her body, and he wondered if they were tears of joy or anguish … but he dared not look, or ask which it was.

With their horses packed up, saddlebags and blanket rolls put in place, Simms slid the Halls into its scabbard and lit a rare cigarette whilst waiting for the operator to return with the message from Bridger. Beside him, White Dove, dressed in buckskins, a gun belt tied tight to her waist, studied the Navy Colt Masterson given to her as a present. She ideally rotated the cylinder. When she caught Simms studying her, her cheeks reddened.

"Let's hope you don't need it."

"Hope is not something to rely on."

"Maybe not, but we take it slow and careful. It'll take us an extra day to skirt the town and come at it from the north. We'll be crossing Indian territory, so we can't camp with a fire. They'll be on us like a plague of mosquitoes after blood if we do."

"Perhaps we should not camp at all."

"We'll be dog-tired if we don't. I don't much fancy going up against anyone tired, let alone that wildcat Tabatha."

"You think it is her who sent the telegram?"

"Without a doubt. She has a score to settle. I arrested her mother for a heinous crime, then shot her dead when she came at me over at Masterson's."

"I saw his face when you mentioned what happened. Full of shame, fear."

"They were going cut his balls off."

Her face remained impassive. "What would they have done to you?"

"God knows. A whole lot worse, I reckon. Least ways, I shot the mother and Tabatha made a run for it. I always knew the day would come when we'd end it."

"But this is not something she could do on her own. She must have help."

"Yes, but what sort of help God alone knows. Whatever it is, you can bet it's pretty good and pretty mean. We ain't going into no negotiations, White Dove. Not with her. We see her, we shoot."

"I know." She dropped the Navy into its holster. "And I will shoot, do not fear."

"I have no fear with you beside me."

"I do not think you have fear any way."

"Fear is a good thing, White Dove. It keeps your senses sharp."

"Fear is something you know much about."

He shrugged, took a final pull on the cigarette and ground it out beneath his boot. "It's something I learned to live with back in Forty-Seven, Eight. War can break a man; it can also make him."

"One day you will tell me about it."

"One day.

"Until then, we put our minds on what awaits us in Glory. You know what you must do and you will do it. I will protect your back."

He went to reply but stopped as the operator from the tele-graph office came sprinting down the street. Gasping, he slowed down and thrust the message into the detective's hand.

"The marshal, man named Dixon, he's gone to Twin Buttes. But there's been more killing."

Simms read the words and let their meaning percolate inside. For a long time he remained silent, then slowly turned to White Dove. "After Glory, we go to Twin Buttes."

"It never ends," she said, her voice low.

"It'll end when it ends," he said, grunted and hauled himself into his saddle. Letting out a long sigh, he nodded a farewell to the operator and took his horse out of the town of Bovey, with White Dove close behind, in silence.

Chapter Thirty-Nine

"I'm not really so sure about all this."

The man behind the desk at the assayer's office sat with the claim forms set out before him, glasses perched on the end of his nose, tracing the words with the point of a sharp pencil.

"It's fairly straightforward," said Dixon. "It's a simple transference."

"I understand it may seem that way from your perspective, but since the recent trouble over this claim, we've taken a much more cautious approach."

"But she's his daughter. Those two villains took the claim through deception and, when they were found out, they took your colleague's life."

"Yes, and that of his family also." The man sat back, eyes continuing to regard the papers. "I'll need her signature on every piece, and an independent witness."

"Every piece?"

The man grunted. "The sheriff would be a suitable counter-signatory."

"But I'm a U.S Marshal, surely I can—"

"Usually, but in this particular instance, as you are so close to the main claimant, the counter-signatory would need to be independent. I can arrange it all with the sheriff, if you so wish?

We could arrange a meeting, here in the office. You, the sheriff, the—"

"No, no," said Dixon and gathered up his hat, "I'll speak to him. Every paper?"

"Every paper." The man brought the papers together and handed them back. "As soon as it's done, the legalities will go ahead almost immediately and the claim will be hers."

"I'm the trustee."

"Yes. As you said earlier. The trustee. Once she signs, the transference will go ahead."

Dixon folded the papers and slipped them back into the thin leather satchel he used to hold them in. He put on his hat, tipped the brim and went out.

He stood just outside the door to the office and looked down the street towards the sheriff's office. Taking in a deep breath, he decided to wander over to the saloon first, in order to conduct his business in more amicable surroundings.

At his desk, Silas ruminated over the papers, staring at them with even more concentration than the assayer had. Standing waiting, Dixon put his hands on his hips and sighed. "He said all you need do is sign."

"And this is what she wants?"

"I wouldn't be here if it wasn't."

Grunting, Silas pulled open the top drawer of his desk and brought out a pen. He studied it. "I'll need ink."

"A pencil will do."

"A pencil?" Another grunt and he rummaged around in the drawer for a few more seconds.

"I can go get some ink if you wish," said Dixon, the edge in his voice more pronounced.

"There was one in here … Damn it, one day I'll get to tidying all of this up. There's so much junk in here I could open up a hardware store."

Dixon turned on his heels and went to the door, yanking it open. "I'll get some ink."

"No, it's here." Silas sat back, grinning in triumph, brandishing a stubby pencil. Licking his lips, he stooped over the papers and, with great care, applied his signature next to every one of Melody Milligan's.

With the final scrawl applied, Silas patted the top sheet, beaming, "There it is, Marshal Dixon. All done and dusted, tied up in a fancy blue ribbon." He pushed the papers across the desk and Dixon picked them up, checking each page before returning them to the satchel. "How is Melody?"

Dixon stopped, catching something in the sheriff's voice. He forced a smile. "Not too good. We still haven't found where those rascals buried her father."

"He can't be far. Unless they didn't bury him. Those coyotes, they will take anything."

"That was my thought also, but I didn't wish to mention such an idea to Melody. She's a mite sensitive."

"Of course. My God, such a thing ..." Silas shook his head. "The whole damned business has left a nasty taste in my mouth. What with the killing, then that Dodd fellow... He said old Dan was his friend, but then he rides out of here as if he were on a mission or some such thing. With the woman and those other three low-lifes. I reckon when he gets back, we may have to confront him over one or two things."

"I reckon so." He tied up the satchel and trucked it under his arm. "Well, I'll go register these then make my way back to the camp, tell Melody the good news."

Doffing his hat, he went outside and crossed the street, making his way directly towards the assayer's office. He rattled on the door, but without success and, when he pressed his face up against the frost glass, it was clear the place was closed. Letting out a long, rattling breath, he put his forehead against the glass and tried to let the stress slip away.

He failed.

Stepping down into the street once more, he wandered over to where his horse waited at the hitching rail and hauled himself into the saddle. Keeping his eyes set straight ahead, he slowly moved out of the town towards the camp.

Chapter Forty

Nothing moved in those grim streets. Glory, a town once filled with the promise of a bright future, seemed consumed by a penetrating gloom, the buildings grey, a smattering of people moving around with somnambulistic slowness.

Simms lowered his field-glasses and chewed at his bottom lip. "I can't see anyone waiting, but that doesn't mean they're not."

"I shall ride in first," said White Dove. "I shall go to your office, just as last time. Watch out for me. When I come out, I shall have in my hand a cloth, or something, which I will wave. It will be safe. If I come out with no cloth, it is not."

Arching a single eyebrow, Simms carefully put the field-glasses back in their case. "That might be dangerous, White Dove. What if you don't come out at all? What if they open up on you as you—"

"Then there will be no doubts. Besides, they do not know me. For all they know, I am just another drifter."

"They'll be suspicious. Indian squaws don't ride through the Territory on their own with a Colt Navy strapped to their side."

"There are more curious things than that lurking in the Territory. You wait and watch. Remember, a cloth in my hand and all is well."

"I'll remember."

She reached across and squeezed his hand resting on the pommel of his saddle. "We make a good team, you and me."

And then she kicked her horse and rode off down the incline towards the trail leading to Glory.

Simms watched and, no matter how hard he tried, could not stop the hammering of his heart against the wall of his chest.

White Dove moved with nonchalant ease and, with few eyes to watch her approach, she felt relaxed as she eased herself from the saddle and stepped up to the sheriff's office door. She went directly to it and rapped on the woodwork with a gloved fist. Nothing stirred from within, so she tried the handle and found, to her surprise, it opened with a loud, teeth-clenching creak.

For a moment she stood, allowing her eyes to adjust to the gloom, then went over to the desk. It was cold inside, the atmosphere depressed, unwelcoming. She shivered and turned.

The man in the doorway was large, bald head titled at an angle, viewing her with some amusement. What irked her more than anything else, however, was the fact his approach went undetected. Life with Simms had made her soft, she chided herself.

"And what can I do for you?" he asked.

"I have a message," she said without hesitation, "for Sheriff Simms."

The man's eyes widened. "Really? And what sort of message might that be?"

"Are you him?"

He chuckled. "No, no. Not me. He's over at the saloon. I'll take you to him if you like."

She went to move forward, but he got there first, his hand streaking out to take the revolver from her hip. "You won't be needing that," he said.

Without a word, she stepped outside with the man close behind. She paused, stretching her arms, palms open.

"You cramped up?"

"Some. I have ridden a long way." She pointed across the street. "Is that the saloon?"

Nodding, he looked down at the revolver in his hand. "I don't think I've ever seen a lady such as yourself, dressed like some rocky-mountain beaver-hunter. All you need is a fur cap and you'd be just like Davy Crockett."

"I do not know him. Is he from this town?"

He laughed. "'fraid not, little lady."

"I need to take some of the messages from the sheriff's desk to show him."

He cocked his head, frowning. "Messages?"

"Yes. I saw some on his desk. The reason I am here. I need to show him a poster. You will allow me to take it to him?"

Studying her for a few moments, chewing away at his bottom lip, she thought for a moment her ruse would fail. She gave him her most disarming smile. "I cannot go anywhere – and you have my gun. I just need the paper."

Grunting, he stepped aside and pushed the door to the office open. He watched her as she slipped inside and crossed to the desk.

Taking her time, she rustled the collection of papers, strewn over the desk. For a moment she considered the empty whisky bottle, wondering if she might be able to repeat her attack back in Bridger, but she immediately dismissed the notion. Seeing the stranger standing there, with her own gun in his big hand, she knew she would never make it. Already his suspicions were developing, the frown on his face deepening.

"You got it?" he snarled.

A little nod and she picked up the top piece of paper. "Here it is," she said, folding it up and putting it into her sleeve, taking as much time as she could.

His impatience snapped at that moment and he stepped forward, crossing the distance between them in a rush. He grabbed her by the arm and pulled her back outside. She tried to resist, tugging away at his hand, but her efforts failed; he was far too strong.

"Don't force me to hurt you," he said through gritted teeth, throwing her over the boardwalk steps to the ground. She rolled over, holding up both her hands.

"What are you doing," she screamed. "I want to see the sheriff!"

"So you shall. I told you – over in the saloon." He stepped over her, the gun coming up, the barrel looming large in front of her. "I don't know who you are, or what you want, but something ain't right with all this."

"It is you who is not right – I came here to talk to the sheriff. I have news for him. About my brother."

"Your brother?" Again the frown, again the mistrust, the disbelief. "Missy, you is talking nothing but bull. I want to know what the hell it is you really want."

"Your balls, you bastard!"

She scrambled to her feet but the man proved too fast. He gripped her by the throat, lifting her as if she was nothing more than a child. She gagged, both hands wrapping around his one, desperate to tear herself free. He lifted her up, feet thrashing, eyes bulging, and he laughed, tilting his head backwards, displaying the blackened stumps of his rotten teeth.

"Proctor," shouted a voice from across the street, "what in the name of God Almighty are you doing?"

The man holding her, the one called Proctor, looked up, his smiled broadening. "Just having some fun, Dodd, that's all."

"Put the girl down and bring her over here to me."

Proctor's eyes settled on White Dove's. "I'm going to beat the truth out of you, little girl. Then I'm gonna have some fun with you."

She croaked, continuing to thrash in his grip, but his fingers, like steel bands, continued to press against her. Her strength drained away, the surroundings growing blurred, her mind a turmoil of confusion and terror. No longer able to breathe, the heat rushed to her face, her eyes, the pulsing of her heartbeat within her head growing so loud, so powerful, it seemed to her it would explode.

Then he released her and she fell, heavy and limp, to the ground where she lay, gasping, clutching at the rawness of her throat, whimpering.

"Bring her over here," came the voice again. She heard it as if in a tunnel, the sound like an echo coming from deep within a distant cave.

Then rough hands were lifting her again and she stood, rocking, unstable, strength slowly returning.

And the focus of her eyes.

His face, still grinning.

Proctor. She would remember that name.

"Now get moving," he said and prepared to thrust out his hand to push her towards the other man across the street.

But he never did.

A great burst of blood, brain and skull fragments erupted from the left side of his head, quickly followed by the explosion of a gunshot.

Even before the man pitched over, White Dove was running, sweeping up the dead man's gun and making straight for the sheriff's office, legs still unstable, moving like a drunkard but elated her saviour had at last come.

Simms.

A bullet smacked into the door as she hurled herself at it and plunged inside. She sprawled across the floor and rolled over onto her back in time to see the man on the far side of the street retreating into the saloon as the sound of pounding hooves drew ever closer.

And then the horse reining in outside, the sound of his boots on the boardwalk.

And then she fell into unconsciousness.

Chapter Forty-One

Simms put a chair against the broken door, got down next to White Dove and lifted her head. He gently trickled water from his canteen over her lips and she spluttered and coughed, senses returning.

"Oh my love," she croaked, the sinews in her neck straining, red raw.

"Don't speak," he said, applying his dampened bandana around her neck. "Just lie there, take your time."

"I thought you would never come," she managed, her voice rasping, like nails raking across stones. She winced and coughed again.

"I said don't talk. I'm here now. I had to get within range for the Halls to take that bastard out. I'm sorry I couldn't stop him from hurting you."

Her eyes creased and she gripped his hand with her own.

He leaned forward and kissed her forehead.

"You stay here, drink slowly from this," he shook the canteen in front of her, "and don't come out until I tell you it's safe."

"But—"

He put his forefinger over her lips. "No talking. Rest. You have the Navy and you shoot anyone who comes through that door. Put the chair up against it when I leave."

Moving away, her put another paper cartridge into the breach of the Halls carbine, pulled back the chair and went outside in a crouch, weaving left and right.

She strained her head to watch, but he was gone and all she could do was sigh.

* * *

Simms knew the saloon well. The shootout with Shelby and his associates only months before continued to play itself out in his mind as he sprinted across the street to the narrow alleyway running alongside the building. He flattened himself against the wall, breathing hard. Snapping his head to his right, he saw the side entrance, which led into the store room behind the main bar. Inside were kept the many barrels and bottles which provided the saloon's customers with their drinks. One of his adversaries lay dead in the street, and the other, who stood and fired his revolver with such precision, was now inside. How many more, he asked himself? And where was Tabatha?

Sucking in a breath, he edged his way along the wall, the Halls primed and ready, keeping his advance towards the door slow and careful. All the while he strained to hear any signs of movement from within, but there was nothing.

At the door he stopped and stepped away to look up. The upper storey windows glared back at him, black and empty.

Except for one.

The sash was open and he felt sure a shadow flittered across it.

He slammed himself back against the wall, settling his breathing, sensing rather than hearing someone above him, someone with a gun, waiting to take a pot-shot.

With a decisive step into the open, he swung the Halls towards the open window.

And saw him.

A man, his thin white face split into a grin, the revolver streaking out before him.

Simms put a bullet into the man's gaping mouth, blasting him backwards into the room.

Even before the echo of the gunshot drifted away, Simms put aside the carbine, went to the door and kicked it open, the twin Patersons in his hands.

Another man came out from behind the stacks of barrels and crates, the whites of his eyes shining bright in the gloom.

Already Simms was rolling, the first shots from his assailant's gun blasting through the open door. Reaching a stack of barrels, Simms loosed off a shot in the man's general direction, but then he was fleeing, tearing open the door leading into the saloon. Simms sent another shot through the door, the bullet winging the retreating man high on the shoulder, sending him forward on his face.

Not waiting, Simms ran back outside, knowing they would be in the saloon, crouched behind upturned tables, preparing to send a fusillade of gunfire into him as he stepped into the saloon proper. So he scooted back the way he came, returning to the street and the main entrance to the saloon. He saw the bat-wing doors burst open and the gunman stagger out, hand clutching his shoulder, shouting, "Sean? Sean where are you? Answer me, goddamn it!"

So Simms decided to answer for him, stepping out, eyes centred on the entrance. "Over here, son."

The gunman reacted, swinging around towards the direction of Simms' voice, and Simms put two bullets into his chest. Eyes wide with anguish and shock, the gunman teetered backwards along the boardwalk and Simms sent him on his way with another shot through the head.

Each Patterson revolver held five shots in its cylinder. Simms took a moment to count how many he had remaining. The Halls lay in the side alley. There was no time to reload, for the man who had fired at White Dove, and thankfully missed, now stepped out into the sunlight.

A tall man dressed in pin-stripe trousers, pristine white shirt and silver threaded waistcoat. At his hip was a holstered Navy Colt.

"You must be Simms," he said.

A nod sufficed for a reply.

"I'm going to shoot out your balls. The little lady inside wants the pleasure of killing you."

"Then best get to doing it."

The slightest of flickering across the eyes, then Dodd went for his gun in a blur.

He may have been one of the fastest Simms had ever known. He may also have been one of the most proficient of gunmen.

But Simms brought up his gun with equal swiftness and put three bullets into him. His last three bullets sent the man called Dodd into a sort of jig, his feet slipping on the steps, all control gone. Everything gone.

Simms released a long breath and took a step closer, the Patersons smoking in his hand. Dodd, sprawled out in the dirt, eyes open in a look of abject disbelief, was dead. Turning his head, the detective saw the other dead bodies; he slowly ticked them off, making a mental tally, including the one shot in the bedroom. A heaviness pressed down upon him, the shame of it.

A despairing acceptance ran through him that there was one more to account for. He doubted he possessed the stomach for it. Tabatha. He eased the twin Patersons into their holsters and stared at his trembling hand. To kill a woman. This was not something he had deliberately done before. There was Tabatha's mother, of course, shooting her dead in Martinson's shop, but that was different. She was out of control, intent on killing *him*. But Tabatha. They had shared affection, despite Simms using her, knowing she was only surrendering to him to lure him into her trap. A trap to murder him. And yet, to premeditate, to plan, to consciously take her life...

The thin click of a gun hammer engaging cut through his thoughts; he felt his stomach pitch over. Cursing himself he turned his head to see her, standing some hundred feet away, the rifle in her hand, pointing unerringly towards him. He closed his eyes for a moment.

"I counted the bullets, detective," Tabatha said, her voice eerily calm. "I know you have no more in either of your guns."

His shoulders sagged, knowing the truth of her words. For a moment, he contemplated making a dive across the ground, to give himself a chance of dodging the bullet, but he knew he would be dead before he took the first step. More than once Tabatha had demonstrated her skill with a weapon. Resigned, he turned to face her, controlling his breathing, watching her walking in grim determination towards him, her face set in a maniacal grin, eyes full of venom and hate.

"I've waited a long time for this," she said.

"You miss with that rifle, I'll finish this. I'll get my hands around your neck and—"

A soft chuckle, "I have one of Dodd's six-guns, detective. I'm going to fill you so full of lead they'll be able to use you as a colander back in that restaurant I used to work at in Twin Buttes." Another laugh, more of a cackle this time. She tilted her head and gazed at the body sprawled out some feet away from where Simms stood. "I didn't think you'd get the better of Dodd," she continued; Simms thought he heard a tinge of regret in her voice. "Looks like you are better than I ever gave you credit for."

"Why not just put the gun down, then we can—"

"What, take up our love affair before you drag me back to Bovey to face trial? I don't think so." She raised the rifle again, fitting the stock into her shoulder. Closing one eye, she squinted down the barrel. "I'll take out your legs first, then enjoy myself with the rest of you. I want you to suffer for all the pain you brought me, you cold-hearted bastard."

"For all the pain I caused *you*? What about what you were going to do to Martinson?"

"That was a little bit of fun, before you shot my mother dead."

"She was a murderer. Like all of you – killing those others out on the range, to eat them, you sick, depraved bunch of wretches."

"I am a wretch, you're right. But, as the good hymn says, I'll be saved, because I am the Way of the Lord. And I have come down to bring His wrath upon you, Simms, for what you did. Now, say your own prayers, because your life is all petered out."

Her grin widened. Simms held his breath. The seconds crawled by.

Then he saw it, a shadow emerging from the side street between the saloon and the other buildings.

Tabatha noticed it too. She paused and frowned, moving her head slightly towards the direction of the movement. A tiny yelp of fear escaped from between her lips.

White Dove held the revolver in two hands, dead straight, unerring, the hammer engaged. She fired the shots in slow, deliberate fashion, ensuring each bullet hit its mark, slamming into Tabatha's body, sending her into a frenzied dance of death, legs losing control, body crumpling, spewing blood, hitting the ground. She writhed there, limbs thrashing wildly, the blood bubbling from the holes in her chest, squeals of despair ringing out across the street.

She then grew still. Dead.

They commandeered a flat wagon into which they dumped the bodies. No words passed between them, White Dove acting as if nothing had happened, Simms not knowing what to say. As they draped the last of the bodies, that of Tabatha, over the rest, Simms leaned against the tailgate and dragged a hand across his brow. "Nothing I can say will ever be enough to tell you how—"

She held up her hand and stepped closer. She had not even broken into a sweat. "There is no need." Her palm rested against his cheek. "I am yours now." Smiling, she leaned into him and kissed him tenderly on the lips.

Chapter Forty-Two

Having left the bodies back in Bovey and, with the paperwork duly completed, Simms rode off towards Twin Buttes. White Dove begged him to allow her to accompany him, but this time Simms' insistence she stay behind won through.

He rode hard, taking only short stops to allow his horse to recover, easing off its saddle, wiping her down, feeding her oats whilst he himself partook of salt-biscuits and gulps of water. Within two days he made the town limits, reining in on a rise to study the outline of the place.

Like so many other towns, Twin Buttes was more of a mixed up, ill-thought out sprawl, buildings erected in haste to accommodate miners and prospectors come to find their fortune in the gold seams of the surrounding mountains. There was a church, perhaps the best preserved of all the structures, with a bell tower. A good place to look out for any approaching danger.

Sucking in his lips, Simms reached for his saddle bag and tugged out the field-glasses. Of German manufacture, the lenses were of the finest quality, allowing him a clear view of the streets, the people crossing backwards and forwards, and the bell tower.

There was a man.

In his hands, distinct and unmistakable, a rifle.

For a moment, a memory of Beaudelaire Talpas came into the detective's mind. A sharpshooter of the very highest calibre, Talpas could take out a man's eye at over five hundred paces, hit him anywhere at a thousand. Could this be a similar marksman?

Simms lowered the glasses and slowly dismounted.

He settled himself down amongst the rocks, tying up his horse to a nearby tree. He sat with his back against a rock, pulled his hat over his eyes and relaxed. When night fell, he would move into the town of Twin Buttes and find out just what the hell was going on.

Stomping his feet upon the boardwalk, Silas shrugged off his overcoat and shook it. The rain pounded down and already he was soaked through. He took a quick look across the deserted street, did his best to lift his depressed mood and went through the door.

He froze in the doorway.

Behind his desk, feet propped on the desk, hat pulled down over his eyes, sat a wiry individual, grizzled chin, a Colt Navy resting within reach. He smiled as Silas gaped.

"Who in the name of God are—"

"Simms," said the man. "The name is Simms – Pinkerton detective, out of Bovey."

Silas continued to gawp at this stranger. There was something in his demeanour which reminded him of Dodd, the gunfighter. An air of menace, just under the surface. A man not to be trifled with,

"Why in the hell are you in my office, God damn you?"

"It was raining. Thought I'd take shelter. And the door was open…" He shrugged and stood, picking up the Navy and dropping it into the holster at his hip. With his eyes locked on Silas, he moved, almost glided, across to the wood burner. On the hot plate stood a pot, its contents gently bubbling, dribbles of dark brown liquid coming out of the spout. "Coffee?"

Silas took a deep breath. "Mister, would you kindly tell me what it is you want – taking shelter from the elements notwithstanding."

Simms poured coffee into two chipped enamel cups. He took a moment to breathe in the aroma before handing one across to Silas, who took it, frowning.

"I hear you've been having some trouble."

Silas paused in the action of taking a sip. His frown deepened. "We *had* some trouble. It's all sorted now."

"Ah." Simms drank and nodded with satisfaction. "So, a U.S. Marshal did finally come?"

"He did – but the trouble was sorted before he arrived."

"And where might he be now?"

"I … I don't rightly know. Over at his claim I shouldn't wonder."

"His claim?"

"Mister, I don't think any of this is your business. I'm sheriff of this town and it'll be me who—"

"Oh, it's my business all right, Sheriff. This marshal. His name is Dixon?"

"How in the hell—"

"Like I said, I'm a Pinkerton."

"I have no idea what that means."

"Well, you do now. I'm a lawman, like yourself. I'm here to apprehend this Dixon character. He's wanted in Bridger for attempted fraud and … " He took a sip of his coffee, "murder."

"Jesus." Silas pressed the door closed and crossed to his desk, laying the cup down on the surface. He pulled off his sopping hat and ran a hand through his hair. "And you know this for a fact?" Simms nodded. "I'll need to see your badge, mister. Not that I'm doubting you, but—"

Without a moment's hesitation, Simms eased back his coat to reveal his sheriff's badge. "I'm also sheriff of Glory. There was some trouble over there which I had to fix before making my way here."

"Trouble? Wait, wait a minute..." Silas leaned back against the edge of his desk, his breathing growing ragged. "Jesus ... Glory? Are you ... Dear God ... Dodd, and the woman, they ... Oh my God ..."

Placing his cup down next to the sheriff's, Simms buttoned up his coat. "Yeah."

"And you ... You and Dodd?"

"The woman too."

"But he had men with him. Proctor and those two—"

"They won't be troubling anybody anymore ... 'cept maybe the undertaker."

"You mean...?" His face took on a pained expression and he stumbled to the other side of the desk, where he collapsed into his chair. "Dear God, I never believed ... You shot Dodd? How in the hell did you manage that?"

"With three bullets. Listen sheriff, I want you to tell me, real truthful like, why this Marshall Dixon is sitting up in the church bell tower with a rifle."

"Why he's ... ?" Silas shook his head, bemused. "What the hell do you mean?"

"What I say. Take your time, but make sure it's the truth. My patience has almost all run out."

"Mister, I – I honestly don't know. As far as I knew he was at the claim with that woman of his."

"Woman?"

"Yes, some pretty little thing she was. Mighty pretty."

"Small, honey coloured hair, eyes as big as a doe's?"

"Yes, yes, that could be her."

"Her name, you know her name?"

"No, but she said – well, *Dixon* said she was here to find her father. Dan Stoakes."

Simms moved, his hand coming up in a blur, the Navy held straight out, hammer engaged. "Tell me quick, Sheriff, or I'll blow your fucking head off. *Why is that bastard in the bell tower*?"

Silas groaned, blood draining from his face. His mouth fell open, close to losing control. His hands reached up high towards the ceiling, "Oh sweet Jesus, mister, *I don't know.* I swear to God."

Simms nodded towards a door to the rear of the office. "Where does that lead?"

"Back alley. Mister, I truly don't know what the hell this is all about. As far as I knew, Dixon and the girl, they were planning on taking over her father's claim. There is a little shack up there and I assumed they would make something of it whilst they mined the silver old Dan found. That's the truth of it, I swear to God."

"If you're lying, I'll be back, and I'll kill you."

"Please, mister, I'm not lying. Dixon, he seemed like a decent enough fella, and the girl seemed real fine, no side to her. No side to either of 'em. Just ordinary folk, I guess. Sure, he was a marshal, but with the trouble all sorted, I guessed he might make a go of it here, with her."

"And he said nothing about wanting to take a shot at me?"

"No – nothing at all. That was Dodd, the gunfighter. Dodd and the woman. They said they was going to Glory to—"

"I told you that was all fixed." He blew out a breath and dropped the Navy into its holster. "Now I have to fix this."

Visibly relaxing, Silas slowly lowered his hands. "The girl, she seemed sick. Fever, I reckon."

Simms winced at the words. "Fever."

"She seemed mighty sick. Listen, if you need any help, I'll be willing to lend you a hand."

Tilting his head, Simms' expression changed to one of mild amusement and he sniffed loudly. "Mister, I think first you'll be needing a bath."

And with that, he left by the back door.

Silas sat and watched, torn between anger and shame, but above all else, experiencing an overwhelming sense of relief. He had stared death in the face and survived. It was not something he ever wanted to repeat.

Chapter Forty-Three

The inside of the church smelled of damp and wood rot. Standing just inside the doorway, having approached the building from the side and keeping himself low, Simms surveyed the empty pews, the simple decorations and the cloth covered altar at the far end. He eased back the hammer of the Colt, the mechanism resounding loud around the empty space as if it were the onset of a symphony orchestra. Wincing, he waited, ears straining for the slightest sound.

Nothing stirred.

Taking his time, easing one foot after the other, always alert for any movement or sound, Simms moved down the central aisle. At the far end, behind a stone font, the bell ropes dangled from the open entrance to the tower far above. When he reached them, he peered upwards, expecting at any moment a figure to appear, rifle in hand.

Again, nothing moved.

A worn and unsafe spiral staircase went up to the void above and he slowly climbed, the Navy ready, his mouth open, breath shallow and light.

Each step took an age.

Every now and then he would stop, senses alert, listening. At the top, he paused, gathering himself. If anyone waited there, now would be the moment to attack. No attack came and he peeked out into the tiny loft, the single bell hanging there, large and silent. Nothing else. No sharpshooter, no sign of anyone...except...

He squinted over to the open window, where Dixon had waited. The void would give a commanding view over the approach road to the town.

Dropping the Navy into its holster, he put his palms flat on the floorboards and hauled himself into the space.

Keeping low, he went over to the open window and looked out along the southern approach road, the exact same one he would have ridden along if he had not stopped and trained his field-glasses on this strange and silent town.

At the foot of the window, where Dixon had stood, he saw the dead butts of three cigarettes. He recalled seeing Dixon smoking back at Bridger. The Marshal must have waited here for a long time for Simms to show. And now he was gone.

There could only be one place.

At the old mine, the one where Dan Stoakes discovered the silver lode which would have resulted in great riches for him and his surviving family, Simms eased himself from his saddle, taking his time to scan the old workings.

Abandoned, it oozed with an air of depression, disappointment and crushing loneliness. He traced the line of the stakes, the scratched out declaration of the claim, Dan's name, the date...

In the collapsed, broken down old tent, he rummaged through the meagre remains of the miner's life. An old blanket, some dried out tobacco, shovels, picks, a single boot.

Never a tracker, he nevertheless followed the claim further along the line of the stream running alongside, finding the imprints of booted feet with ease. There was blood too, and what he believed to be traces of black powder. Someone had fired guns here. But who?

Getting down on his haunches, he pulled out his gun and listened. The river trickled by, water running over rocks, its course swift and relentless. But nothing else.

Apart from that same heavy, depressed atmosphere. Filled with foreboding, he crept forward.

The rundown old shack stood in a small clearing, bordered by wild, unkempt bushes of gorse and twisted, ancient trees, more a jungle of spidery twigs and branches than anything of true form. Everything forgotten, tired, soon to be overgrown, hidden forever.

Reaching the door, he eased back the hammer of his revolver and pushed open the rickety entrance, set on a single, rusted hinge. It creaked open, setting his teeth on edge.

He saw her straight away, a shaft of light from the open doorway bathing her in an eerie, otherworld glare. Propped up in the corner, she sat, staring into the distance, the luster of her eyes now gone, skin waxy and grey. A thin trickle of dried blood trailed from the corner of her blued lips.

Melody Milligan, the girl he spoke to at Deep Water's home. The girl afraid, recovering from her ordeal at the hand of the Indians Deep Water had rescued her from.

Dead.

Simms groaned and swung out of the doorway, falling back against the wall of the shack. For a long time he sat, not thinking, numb, not knowing what to do.

At last, some time later, he forced himself to go inside, stretching out his hand to check her pulse. He knew even before his fingers touched her cold flesh he would feel nothing. He brushed his hand over her face and closed her eyelids. Then, as he went to move back outside, he saw them. Those damning bits of evidence, the same as in the belfry.

Cigarette butts.

He took in a sharp breath, biting down on his bottom lip, the fury welling up from deep within.

Dixon.

Yet another to add to his list. A list he felt sure would never come to an end, but one which would forever grow longer and longer still.

He bunched his hand into a fist and decided to set off to find Deep Water. If anyone could find the ruthless lawman, it was the Indian tracker, the best Simms knew.

Dipping low, he stepped through the door.

And there he was.

For a moment it seemed as if the world had ceased to turn; that the birds, the trees, the sky and the river were all frozen in a grip of total terror.

"Hello, Detective."

Those words rang out across the distance between them, like the death knell from a grotesque, gothic church, a black mausoleum of death. An awful, hollow sound, one which sank deep into Simms' soul, causing him to sway backwards slightly, stunned and revolted at the same time.

"I wasn't sure when we'd meet again, but I'm glad the wait is over."

"You killed her, you bastard. You'll pay for that."

"I don't think so, Detective. And, for you information, she died of fever. Struck her down the day after we arrived. I did all I could."

"You're a damn liar."

"Well, say what you like, you ain't gonna be able to prove a damned thing."

"You're going back to Bridger with me to face trial."

Dixon smiled, his eyes narrowing. "No. I'd rather play out my hand here and now, not end up dangling from the end of a rope."

"So be it. Either way, you die."

"You're mighty sure of yourself, ain't you, Detective? You're forgetting, I saw you back in the Fort. I never saw anything that worried me none."

He went for his gun. A Navy Colt, positioned for a cross-belly draw.

Simms shot the gun out of the Marshal's hand, blowing off the first two fingers. Dixon screamed, clutching at his shattered limb with his other hand and Simms shot him again, high up on the left shoulder, spinning him around like a fairground toy. Another scream, high-pitched, and the third bullet hit him in the back of the left thigh, dropping him to his knees.

He knelt there, cradling his hand, the blood pumping over his trembling skin to splatter onto the ground.

Simms strode around to face him. He always kept the hammer resting on an empty chamber, so two bullets remained. He longed for more.

"I'm going to leave you to bleed out, you bastard," said the Pinkerton, "let you get real acquainted with death."

Through trembling lips, Dixon managed a pitiful, "Please…"

Then Simms shot him in the inner thigh of the man's right leg. He keeled over, bunching up his knees, writhing in the dirt, blood leaking from his wounds, eyes screwed up, whimpering with the horror and pain of it all.

Simms picked up the other gun. The bullet, as he suspected, had gone through the casing as well as Dixon's fingers, but nevertheless Simms hurled it high into the air towards the river and waited, listening out for the satisfying splash of its entry.

He dropped his own gun into its holster, strode back to his horse and mounted up. One last look at the still stricken Dixon and he swung away and calmly made his way back to Twin Buttes.

His work done.

She waited for him outside the doorway to the ranch, broom in hand, her face split in a grin as wide as a half moon. They ran to one another and he caught her by the waist and spun her around, both of them laughing.

Back on her feet, her eyes roamed over him, his face and upper body receiving particular attention. "Are you sure you're not hurt?"

"Not a scratch. But Melody …" He looked away, eyes brimming, "Deep Water won't take it well. I have a notion he was kinda sweet on her."

"That poor girl, to have lost everything. That man, that marshal, he …?"

He nodded, no words necessary. He snaked his arm around her waist and together they strolled back to the house. "You've made it look all homely," he said, unable to keep the emotion from his voice.

"Because that is what it is," she said and stopped, reaching up to take him by the neck. She kissed him. "It is our home."

Dear reader,

We hope you enjoyed reading *A Reckoning*. Please take a moment to leave a review, even if it's a short one. Your opinion is important to us.

Discover more books by Stuart G. Yates at
https://www.nextchapter.pub/authors/stuart-g-yates

Want to know when one of our books is free or discounted? Join the newsletter at http://eepurl.com/bqqB3H

Best regards,

Stuart G. Yates and the Next Chapter Team

The story continues in:
Blood Rise by Stuart G. Yates

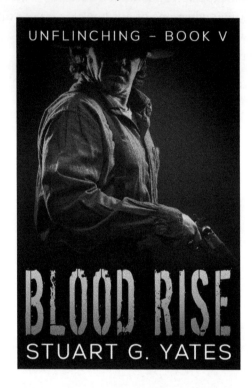

To read the first chapter for free, head to:
https://www.nextchapter.pub/books/blood-rise

About the Author

Stuart G Yates is the author of a eclectic mix of books, ranging from historical fiction through to contemporary thrillers. Hailing from Merseyside, he now lives in southern Spain, where he teaches history, but dreams of living on a narrowboat in Shropshire.